LOVE, PASSION AND HATE

A Faithful Choice 2

By

Theresa Grant

DEDICATION

I dedicate this book to my family and all of my loyal
fan and customers who have stuck with me and
supported me for every book that I have written and
published.

ACKNOWLEDGEMENTS

Thanks to all my teachers and mentors. Hello to all you readers out there. A big thanks to Pam and Chuck Nelson for allowing me to use their picture on the front cover. I hope you are not too shocked by the contents. I worked hard to make it the best it can be, keeping it clean and on everyone's mind. I hope that you will find something to keep turning the pages. Finally, I'd like to thank all of you who have been reading my books, and a special thanks to those of you who have been writing to me through my web site and telling me how much you have enjoyed my blogs. It means a lot to me.

1 LOVE, PASSION AND HATE

A Faithful Choice 2

CHAPTER 1

Dolores and Sonny's plane landed in Paris at the Charles de Gaulle Airport, also known as Roissy because it is located in the northern suburb by that name. They headed to terminal number one and out to their limousine. "Where is Maurice? Didn't you tell him to meet us?"

"I thought you took care of those arrangements." Sonny searched the waiting cars looking for some sign of a short, honey colored man with a dark short beard connected to his sideburns and wearing a gray chauffeur's uniform. "Maurice isn't among these guys."

She rolled her eyes at him and clamped her lips together. "You mean no one knew our schedule?"

"Not if you didn't notify them." He doubled back and stood in the center of the cars. "There is no sign of Maurice."

"Never mind," She uttered with annoyance. "We'll just rent a limo. See to the luggage."

"Yes, Madame. At your command." He stopped for a moment, smiled and kissed her cheek.

She blushed, inhaled through her nose andexhaled. "C'mon and stop joshing."

They got a limousine and headed for her château. "What a beautiful April day." She felt blissfully happy and fully alive as she peered out of the limousine's window. "It's mild, sunny, slightly breezy and with a tinged of melancholy in the air."

He smiled and patted her shoulder. "Couldn't ask for a better day."

They arrived at the château and Dolores placed a call to Michelle. "We're here, in Paris."

"Mom? I wanted to meet you at the airport."

"Your father ruined that for you, Michelle." She gazed at Sonny and rolled her eyes upward.

"I'm on my way. I'll tell the others."

"I feel happy to be here." He moved to the bedroom, watched Dolores as she opened one of the leaded windows and inhaled when he felt a cool breeze flutter inside.

Dolores peered out at the silvery poplar trees and shimmering green lawn. "This garden always fascinated me." Her memory drifted back to the days she and Leonard had spent there and she remembered how he complimented her landscaping techniques after she'd planted a dozen pink rose bushes, added a splashing fountain and a lush assortment of small trees. She had marveled at the surprise in his eyes after she

2

added flowering shrubs and statues of cranes and birds.

A happy smile lit her eyes.

She was suddenly brought back to reality when Michelle rushed through the door and held her in her arms. "Mom, I'm happy to see you and Daddy."

Sonny held her close then headed for the door. "Maurice, bring the luggage inside."

"Remembering the past?" Michelle asked, standing next to her and peering out at the garden. "I remember how Leonard loved this view."

"He gave me everything; love, riches, fame and power. All are now mine to keep."
"Velasco's shops made close to eleven million dollars last year," Michelle stated. "His dream of making the shops bigger and better is a reality."

"Yes and I intend to make sure it stays his way."

Michelle smiled and teased her. "The shops are your passion and your playthings."

"You'd better believe they are especially the Paris and the District of Columbia Stores."

Michelle looked at the expression of satisfaction in her eyes. "Yes, Mom, you've given Leonard his dream."

3

She complimented herself and her accomplishments. "I'm responsible for establishing the two most successful luxury shops in the world's best styles, furs and haute couture."

"Yes, Mom." She wrapped her arms around her. "But try to leave the past behind. You and Daddy deserve to be happy now."

Christy entered and held Dolores in her arms. "Great to see you, Mom." She stood beside her and peered out into the garden. "What a place! It's sheer heaven."

"I've loved Louveciennes since the first time I stood in this spot with Leonard." Dolores held her head high. "It's a beautiful suburb."

"What's going on?" Sonny took Dolores in his arms. "It's time for dancing and planning our wedding."

"Oh, Daddy, I'll arrange everything. You'll have your day."

"I know. Is it any wonder? I'm excited. That will be the happiest day of my life."

"And romantic," Christy added. "There's no place more romantic than Paris."

"Sorry that I have to say hello and run but Eugene and I have to do some shopping. You mind watching the twins?"

"Course not, Michelle. I love having them.

LOVE, PASSION AND HATE

A Faithful Choice 2

"Thanks. See you in a couple of hours. I'll leave my phone here. Mind taking calls?" She kissed the twins and hurried outside.

Several hours later, Dolores answered a call for Michelle. "What? Analoude and Joliet . . a car accident?" She held her heart, took a deep breath and shook her head. "Oh, Lord," she yelled and held on to Sonny. "Call the number Michelle gave us for Eugene."

"You call. I'll go with Maurice to get them. They shouldn't drive."

An hour later, Maurice let them out at the entrance of the American Hospital and they hurried inside clinging to each other. Eugene, half out of his mind with worry, approached the information desk. "Monsieur and Madame Glauert?"

"I'm Doctor Juno Pollack." He extended his hand. "Sorry. Mrs. Galuert died fifteen minutes before you arrived."

Michelle slumped to the floor, while Eugene pounded the hospital's wall with his fist.

Dr. Pollack rushed over to examine her. "Still breathing." He handed an ampule of ammonia to Eugene. "Give her a whiff of this."

5

Michelle opened her eyes. "What are we to do?"

"We'll stay the night," Eugene said and lifted her from the floor. Stark and vivid fear gleamed in his eyes. "Dad will get well. He's strong."

Michelle couldn't stop crying. "I can't believe this happened. Joliet is a good driver."

Eugene put his arms around her. "It may not have been his fault."

"Mr. Glauert is in ICU," Dr. Pollack said. "He's in a coma."

Nine o'clock the next morning, Michelle answered her cell phone. She sobbed into Dolores' ear, "They're gone, Mom. Joliet died, during the early morning, while Eugene and I watched."

"I'm sorry, Michelle." She turned and whispered to Sonny, "Don't let the children hear this. Their grandparents are dead." She continued with Michelle. "What can we do?"

"I'm waiting for them to release the bodies. We'll be home soon." She felt as though she was caught up in some kind of dream or nightmare.

"Don't worry. I know the funeral will be huge but your father and I will help."

"People will come from the little town of Ramboulluiet, not to mention the Chevreuse Valley." Hot tears rolled down her cheeks and Eugene wiped them with his fingers. "I can't handle this alone."

"You won't have to." Dolores said. "Your father and I will take care of the flowers."

"Analoude loved fresh flowers." She remembered the fragrant scent of the flowers. "Get Coronations from La Cite, her favorite flower market."

On a somber, gray rainy day, on the family estate in Chevreuse, fifty mourners from the Chevreuse Valley stood shoulder to shoulder with the fifty from Rambouillet. Everyone said their goodbyes and placed a single rose on each coffin.

For the next few weeks, thereafter, Eugene spent most of his time at the mill. He came home long after Michelle had retired and left before she had awakened. She phoned Dolores. "Hi, Mom, guess what?

"What's wrong?" She braced herself for more bad news.

"When I rolled over in bed, that husband of mine had left." A powerful sense of irritation riveted her.

"Go back to sleep, Michelle. Get some rest."

"I'll try." She put the phone back into its receiver, wrapped herself in the covers and slept until noon. She awoke nauseous and vomited. She phoned

Dolores. "I'm sick. I need a doctor."

"I'll drive you. Wait for me." She hurried out of bed and alerted Sonny. "Start the Mercedes. Michelle needs me."

An hour later, in Doctor Bernard's office, Michelle heard the results of his examination and diagnosis.

"You're two months pregnant."

Michelle almost fell off of her seat. "Another baby? I have six year old twins. How am I going to tell Eugene? God, this is real. It's all so real."

They left the doctor's office and Dolores drove home to tell Sonny the good news.

"For every life lost, another takes its place," Sonny said and embraced Michelle. "You're quite the little mother." He kissed her cheek. "You make us proud."

Join us for lunch in the dining room. I want to hear what the proud poppa thinks."

"Eugene doesn't know yet. I'm going to surprise him tonight."

They sat on the blue and white satin sofa and ate baked salmon marinated in white wine sauce and talked about the baby. The clock in the hall chimed and Michelle grew anxious. "It's six o'clock. Got to cook."

LOVE, PASSION AND HATE

A Faithful choice 2

"Let's do this together," Dolores suggested. "You must rest. I'll help." She gathered her night clothes and an extra pair of pants and a blouse.

When Dolores and Michelle arrived at her house, Eugene wasn't home. They could hear the laughter of Sherrie and Eugene Jr., in the family room, and it brought a happy smile to their faces. They hurried inside. Michelle stole two quick kisses. "What are you two doing?"

"I have a paper to write for tomorrow's French history class," Sherrie answered. "I'm in college now."

"I can't believe my grand-daughter is attending the University of Paris," The strong sense of family made Dolores feel blessed. "It seems only yesterday when I held you on my knee."

"Oh, Grand-mamma, I'm a senior in college. Not a little girl any longer."

"You're still my little girl, no matter how old you become."

Michelle and Dolores went to the kitchen and began preparing dinner. The maid entered to clean, and Michelle raised her hand. "I won't need you tonight, Simone. You may retire, after you put the twins to bed. Put my black negligee' on my bed. I want to be alone when Mr. Glauert returns home."

"Yes, Madame. I'll help them with their bath

first."

Michelle removed the meat from the freezer. "Let's prepare veal, potatoes with parsley, carrot salad and your apple pie recipe. It's Eugene's favorite."

"I'm happy he likes the apple pie, but it was Mama Kate's recipe." She sighed and a tear came into her eye as she reminisced. She dried the tear and said, "Set the table with white linen and blue china. A little candlelight won't hurt."

Eugene came home at midnight. Michelle was angry and an argument ensued.

"I'm going to bed. Settle your business." Dolores shut her door but she could hear Eugene pleading.

"Michelle, what's wrong? Why're you up so late? Let's go to bed, please."

"I prepared a special dinner for us as a surprise," She raised her fist. "Did you appreciate it? No!"

"I'm sorry, darling. I had no idea. I ate earlier, but what's the surprise?"

"I'm pregnant."

Dolores listened to the silence, until Michelle

burst into her room.

"Mom, you should've seen his face. It twisted and his eyes dilated. They turned misty brown and he made sounds of a chocking person."

His voice had gotten shaky. He cleared his throat. "Uh, all right, huh, I'm happy," he said, standing in the doorway. "It was a shock and a surprise." He hated hurting his wife but he felt sick inside.

The look on his face tore at her heart. "Sure. Your enthusiasm is overwhelming." She ran past him to their bedroom.

He ran after her with Dolores following him.

"I'm not against another baby but we may be in serious financial trouble."

Michelle forgot her anger and became fearful. "What happened?" Her words sounded shaky and she held onto Dolores.

In his despair, he confessed. "I invested in oil and bought into Martin's company."

"How could you do such a thing without discussing it with me?" She screamed at him and slapped him on his head. "How dare you take such an

11

idiotic chance."

A look of indignation enveloped his face. His eyes darkened and he sighed heavily. "I dreaded telling you for fear of how you're acting at this moment." He took her hand in his. "Martin's mill is larger than ours. I wanted to get into manufacturing full scale, supplying fabrics the world over."

She shook her head and stared at him as if he had lost his mind. "No. Your mother and father worked hard for our mill. They did well, though it's small."

"God help me, I know, but I have to trust Martin's financial ability to get us back in the black."

Michelle's mouth opened in dismay and she flung her hands in air. "If he doesn't, can you borrow from the bank?"

He shook his head, shoved his hands in his pocket and hunched his shoulders forward. "That's out. I mortgaged the mill to pay some debts."

She closed her eyes and tears, which must have been hot, trickled down her face like scalding water, searing her light beige makeup, and leaving an ashy line. "I can't believe this is happening. After all we've been through."

"Please, Michelle, calm down. I'll think of something to make this right." She made him feel stupid.

LOVE, PASSION AND HATE

A Faithful Choice 2

They talked until two a.m. and ended up going to bed exhausted. Later that morning, during breakfast, Martin came to the house. Simone let him enter and showed him to the dining room. "Martin, buddy, are you playing hooky from the mill?" Eugene laughed and slapped his shoulder. "Take a seat. Have some breakfast."

Martin didn't crack a smile. He took a seat in the gold, brocaded chair and pulled himself up to the large, French mahogany table. His hands shook and he appeared nervous.

"Something's wrong? You look bad, man. Want some coffee?"

"Whiskey," He insisted with impatience and shaking his hands. "I'm in terrible trouble."

Eugene rushed to the buffet, pressed a button and the mahogany bar spun around in the space where the cabinet stood. He poured a glass of bourbon and handed it to him.

Martin raised the glass to his trembling lips, swallowed the whiskey, in two gulps, and wiped his mouth on the back of his hand. Sweat poured down his bald head and the sides of his round face and wetted his short black beard. He explained his dilemma. "I owe the bank fifty thousand dollars. I can't pull out of this debt."

13

Dolores gasps and yelled, "Oh, Lord."

Michelle bowed her head and squeezed her eyes shut. "I knew this would happen."

Eugene lowered his head on the table. "I'm ruined. I have no money left."

Michelle raised his head, gazed at her man's face and her heart must have ached for him. Then the idea came to her mind. "Mom, can you and Daddy help us?"

"I'm sure we can but let's ask Sonny first." Dolores answered.

Martin's eyes displayed a ray of hope. He put his hand on Eugene's arm. "Tell him about me."

Eugene gazed at Martin. "I don't like asking Sonny. I've always been my own man."

"Put aside your pride, please." He wrung his hands and paced back and forth. "Do this for the business. You'll double your money."

Eugene cleared his throat and agreed. "We can go over and talk to him. Here's the address."

This means a lot to me, man. You're saving the mill."

When Martin left, Eugene went to the den and flopped on the sofa. "I can't let the workers

14

know what may happen, not yet."

Michelle sat beside him, put her arms around his shoulders and her head next to his.

"We've nothing left, except this house and Dad's home. Never did I think we'd come to this." Today, he wasn't sure of anything. "I'll call your father and let him know we're coming."

LOVE, PASSION AND HATE

A Faithful Choice 2

CHAPTER 2

Two hours later, sitting in Dolores' chateau, Martin began his pitch for a loan. "Failure to make our bank loan means foreclosure of our mill. You can join our company with a loan."

Sonny listened. He smiled, removed a cigarette from his golden case, lit it, and responded. "I'm not interested in financing other people's disasters." He drew upon the cigarette and blew a fathom of smoke toward the ceiling. "It doesn't pay. I'll get sacked in the long run."

"Please," Martin shouted, losing his composure. "You'll get interest on every dollar."

Sonny finished his cigarette, doused it in the ash tray and met Martin's dark eyes. "How can I depend on what you're saying? I don't know you."

Eugene say something," Martin beckoned to him. "We're in this together."

Eugene got out of his seat and sat next to Sonny. "Part of this company belongs to Michelle and me. Without your loan, we stand to lose everything."

Sonny turned to Michelle and regarded her quizzically for a moment.

Michelle nodded her head, "Yes."

16

THERESA GRANT

"Ok. We'll buy the company, you manage, but under my control."

Martin exploded. His mouth contorted into an ugly line. He became hysterical, spitting, yelling, "Who in hell is this man? You're crazy. We don't want a take over. We want a loan." He stood there starring at Sonny with hatred in his eyes.

Sonny gave him a cold stare. "You're one crazy mother… beggars have no choice."

Dolores raised her hand. "Please, let's calm ourselves. Isn't the bank taking your company? With us, it'll stay in the family."

Eugene recognized what Sonny was saying. He whispered to Michelle, "Martin lost this company once. He could do so again, the fool." He gave Sonny his answer. "I agree with you. Keeping it in the family is better than letting it go to strangers."

Martin gave him a hard stare and his eyebrows rose in contempt. "All and good for you, but where do I profit? It's all in the family; yours not mine."

Michelle cut in, irritation echoing in her voice. "Wait a minute, Martin; you're the one who screwed this company. All we're trying to do is help you."

"Yeah! You've helped me all right. Out the door."

17

LOVE, PASSION AND HATE

A Faithful Choice 2

"We're offering you a solution," Dolores said. "Accept or decline."

Martin swayed his dark head and shook his fist

at her. "Thank you, but no thanks. I'll go elsewhere."

He got up, gazing at them with cold, bitter hateful eyes. "I'm going to get you for this. You'll be sorry. You bastards." He slammed the door and left.

Dolores rolled her eyes to the ceiling. "Sorry, Eugene, it seems you've lost a friend and we've gained a bitter enemy."

Eugene's face appeared weary and his eyes panic stricken. "It's better this happened now than later." With that, the subject was exhausted, and not another word was exchanged. He took Michelle by the arm and left.

Eugene and Martin tried every bank in town. No one would give them a loan and several weeks later, he and Martin ended up taking Sonny's offer.

Sonny reorganized everything. "I will call this company Brown Enterprises. Eugene will manage and Martin will be the assistant manager."

Michelle thought by Eugene being manager, all of their problems would be solved, but he started working late every night. She and the twins stayed at the chateau with Dolores and Sonny. She was nine months pregnant. Dolores and Sonny assisted her at night, while she slept during the day. Because of night sweats and headaches, she blamed Eugene. "If Eugene was like other husbands, our sexual habits would've been planned. I'm the one suffering."

"Hold on, Michelle," Dolores tried to comfort her. The baby is due any day now."

"Complain, complain, everyday." Sonny shook his head and stared at her. "Nothing consoles her. I don't think she wants this baby."

Dolores defended her. "Eugene thinks he's got to do extra, since Martin isn't doing his part to help. Michelle is disgusted."

Around midnight, after they'd gone to bed, Michelle went into labor. Dolores went to Sonny's room. "Wake up. I heard Michelle groaning."

"Call Doctor Bernard." He yawned and turned over in bed.

Dolores kicked his butt and he jumped out of bed, slid into his trousers and summoned Maurice. "Bring the car around. We're going to the hospital."

Dolores hurried to Michelle. "Easy. We'll get you to the hospital."

"Oh, why is this happening now?" She moaned and held her protruding belly. "Eugene should be here."

19

A Fateful Choice 2

She was feeling more and more uncomfortable. "I want these pains to end now."

"Babies come early in the morning. Don't you remember delivering the twins?" Dolores laughed and helped her into the car.

She frowned and gripped her belly. "The way these pains are hitting me, I'd like to forget. Having my children wasn't fun but I was younger and stronger."

No sooner when Michelle arrived at the hospital, she delivered at three a.m.

"I'll call Eugene," Sonny hurried to use his cell phone in the hospital lobby. He punched the mill's number and the phone rang several times before Eugene answered.

"It's five-thirty a.m. anything wrong?"

"Get your butt over to the hospital. You've got a little girl, born two hours and thirty minutes ago."

Eugene took an hour to get to the hospital. He rushed into Michelle's hospital room. "Thanks for taking care of things."

"No problem, proud poppa." Sonny shook his

hand. "We're family."

Three days later, Sonny and Dolores rode to the hospital with Eugene. "Michelle is being discharged today." He sounded calm and composed but not happy.

When they walked into Michelle's room, she handed the baby to Dolores.

Dolores reached for the baby. "Let me take little . . . what's her name?"

"Grace. It was Eugene's grand-mother's name."

"What a beauty!" Dolores took the baby and kissed her.

They followed Michelle as the nurse pushed her wheelchair outside to the car. Dolores sat in the back seat whispering cute little words to the baby and humming Brahms's Lullaby. Eugene let Sonny out at the chateau and Dolores went home with them to help with the baby.

Michelle immediately wanted to make sure that Eugene would stay home. "We're going to need you with us more than ever. I won't take care of this baby alone."

He gritted his teeth and whipped out the words impatiently. "You have Simone and I'm not on the other side of the world." What more does this woman want from him?

21

LOVE, PASSION AND HATE

A Faithful Choice 2

She snapped at him. "Coming home on weekends isn't enough."

He became frustrated. "We've gone over this situation time and time again. Martin doesn't do much. Everything falls on me to keep the workers straight."

"Martin Fodor will have to be replaced." Her angry voice held venom and like a snake, she hissed at him about Martin. "No one gets a free ride in any of our companies."

Eugene drove into the drive, helped Dolores get the baby inside and went to the den to work on the family's finances.

Michelle and Dolores entered the den with the baby in her arms. Michelle stared at Eugene with a desolate expression. "Did you say goodnight to Valerie and Vilene?"

He avoided her stare and didn't answer.

"Did you hear what I said? The twins are waiting for you to tuck them in."

He slowly turned his head and gazed at her. "What's a man to do? You're knit picking. I've got responsibilities. Don't take that away by forcing me to come home."

"Your first responsibility is here." She held her left breast. "You make my heart ache. The agony of not having you here is tearing us apart." She closed her eyes and said a silent prayer, asking God to help her, to stop her heart from breaking.

He got up from his desk and held his face close to hers till their noses touched. "What do you think it's doing to me? You're not the only person suffering here."

Michelle stormed out of the room, marched into the bedroom and slammed the door. She emerged, ten minutes later, wearing pajamas. She knew how he disliked her wearing pajamas. Then, she got in bed without saying goodnight. She didn't know anything else to do or say to make him change his mind.

Dolores followed Eugene to the den and put sheets on the sofa, after he decided to sleep there. He lay there mumbling. "Our lives have changed since losing my parents and the mill." He shook his head. "This is bad. My wife is unhappy and worst of all, there seems to be no end in sight, unless I have it out with Martin."

"It'll be alright. Give Michelle time. She'll come around."

Eugene fell asleep and awoke at noon. Michelle turned her back, avoided him, and pretended to be busy. He cut his stay short and left Sunday night to go to the

23

mill.

With Eugene away so often, Michelle and the children spent more time at the chateau, leaving her own house early in the morning and returning late at night. One night, as she bundled the children into the car, Dolores made a suggestion. "What's the point of going home? Sherrie and Eugene Jr. are in college. Stay the week."

"Thanks, Mom, your suggestion makes sense."

"Your father and I love having you and the children."

The next Morning, when Michelle had prepared breakfast for everyone, James came home from work. "You look terrible!" She said. "Haven't you had any sleep?"

"No, but thanks for saying I'm a wreck." He acted irritable and appeared unhappy with himself.

"I'm serious," She continued. "I don't like seeing my brother this way."

"I'm working your job at the fashion house, my

24

law practice, plus helping Daddy and Eugene at the mill."

"You've aged; you look older than twenty-four, especially with those dark circles under your eyes." She couldn't hold her tongue. "It won't be long before Grace stops nursing and I'll take over again."

Eugene came home late that night. Michelle exploded. "I expected you earlier."

"I can't see why. There are legal matters at the mill," He said in a flippant tone.

"You can say that and I'd never know what you're doing."

It took a moment to grasp what she meant. It brought him down and killed the good mood that he had created for himself. She watched as his eyes flashed, and his face reddened

He shuddered when he said, "You couldn't be accusing me of what I think you implied."

"I don't know what you thought," She held her eyes shut and opened them to slits. "Maybe your conscious is bothering you." She watched his face as it developed revulsion for himself and for her. He had his hands clenched to his sides and seemed as if he was on the verge of striking her.

"I've never hit a woman in my life and I'm not

about to start now," He said angrily, but you drive a man to those animal thoughts. I have to get out of here. I'm sick of your same old argument."

"You're not leaving!" She yelled. "Come back here, Eugene." The sound of the door slamming exploded in her ears and her eyes filled with tears of helplessness, frustration and rage. She was shocked and humiliated. Never had he walked out on her. She spent the weekend alone, feeling sorry that she had provoked him into leaving and feeling afraid that she had gone too far with him. She telephoned the mill to apologize. "Eugene, I'm sorry. Please forgive me."

"That was a lousy thing for you to say to me." He sighed under his breath. "It was a kick in the gut."

"I didn't mean to hurt you. I love you."

Within minutes, he was responding to her warmth and affection. "There is no one else for me but you. I thought you knew that you're the only woman for me."

"I do. I was angry and I spoke out of anger. I miss having you home."

"It will all be over soon. I'm making headway at the mill. Everything will be as it was when we own the mill." He had to think of someway to get Martin to work. It was either that or he had to force him out.

She finished talking with Eugene and returned

to the kitchen to join Dolores.

"Have a cup of coffee. Your father has eaten and James has gone to work. Let's have a girl talk."

"I want my husband home with me every night. I don't feel married," Michelle admitted. "He's still trying to keep Martin in the business. We don't owe him anything."

"Listen to me, Michelle. You know what he's trying to do. Give him a chance to resolve this thing. Eugene is smart. It'll all be over soon." She put her arm around her. "Sonny and I have been here five months and we haven't planned our wedding."

"I promised to help with this wedding and I'm going to start today. Besides, we have to keep you and Daddy legal." She laughed and hugged her. She hoped and prayed that planning this wedding would keep her mind off of her troubles.

LOVE, PASSION AND HATE

A Faithful Choice 2

CHAPTER 3

"September in Paris. This is a great month for a wedding. Sonny and I have been here six months and he's aching for a wedding."

"I said that I was going to do the honors and I've planned a luxurious wedding and reception with guest for tomorrow." The deep belly laugh she loved filled the room. "Everything is going to be great."

"What? I need my hair done, my nails polished and . . . what time have you selected?"

"It's been a long time coming. Let's get moving. I can't wait another moment to marry your Mama." Sonny was all smiles. He didn't care about time.

Dolores hurried to get her hair done and a manicure. She spent all day preparing for her big day. "I'm glad that I selected my wedding dress before coming to Paris."

The next day, everyone was busy getting ready for the wedding. Dolores rushed to take her shower and to get dressed.

Christy went to look at the rest of the decorations in the chateau and James ran behind her, laughing, until they came to the master bedroom. They sat on the early French canopied bed. James grabbed her derriere. "Let's make fun in here."

Christy laughed gaily as he pushed her down on the bed. "There's no time for this. We have a wedding to attend." She got up and hurried from the room, leaving him on the bed.

The guest started arriving and taking seats in the garden in front of white tents set up with tables and chairs, and decorated with white linens, pink roses, and pink balloons attached to centerpieces on each table. Waiters stood at attention with champagne, while waitresses stood with trays of seafood crepes, assorted pastries, and smoked Nova Scotia Salmon and melon balls for the reception.

Dolores entered wearing a plain, fitted, off the shoulder, white silk dress. A small pill box hat with a short veil matched her dress and white satin shoes with pearls adorned the toes.

Sonny stood next to her dressed in a navy blue suit with a white shirt and black bow tie, a black top hat and white gloves.

Sherrie, looking like an angel, wore a pink organdy dress with puffed, short sleeves, a wide bow tied to her waist, black satin shoes and a Tierra of pink rose buds to hold her hair off of her face. She carried a pink bouquet of roses.

Christy wore a fitted, pink knee length dress cut low in back and a high neckline. She carried pink nosegays and stood next to Dolores as her maid of

LOVE, PASSION AND HATE

A Faithful choice 2

honor.

Eugene Jr., wore a stunning navy blue suit, white shirt and black bow tie.

Eugene Sr. wore the same colors as Sonny and stood next to him as his best man holding Sonny's plain gold band and Dolores' two carat diamond rings.

Dolores and Sonny wrote their own vows. Sonny recited his first, before Pastor Messier, smiling like someone handed him a million dollars. He looked into Dolores' eyes and declared, "You're the only woman I've ever known who gives my life meaning. You've given me another chance. This is a new beginning and I promise to love, honor and cherish you all the days of my life." He placed the rings on Dolores' finger and wiped a tear from his cheek.

Happy tears flooded Dolores' eyes as she said, "We were young and life was a perilous road at times. Now we're older and wiser, and it's time to give life and love another chance. I promise to love, honor and cherish you for the rest of my life." She placed the gold band on his finger.

"I now pronounce you husband and wife," Said Pastor Messier. "You may kiss the bride."

THERESA GRANT

Sonny gave Dolores a long, passionate kiss before everyone rushed to the garden for the reception.

Christy, excited, bounced around like a little kitten. "Where's the honeymoon?"

"We're staying here." Warmth and peace enveloped her heart. "This is as good a place as any for a honeymoon."

"I'll second that motion," Christy said. "Paris was created for lovers."

"Cut the chatter." He took Dolores in his arms. Let's dance, Babe."

Dolores laughed and followed him to the center of the flagstone patio. They danced the first dance before everyone joined them.

Sonny kept his eyes on Dolores. "You're gorgeous, woman. You hear me?"

Smiling, she lifted her face to his. "You're looking handsome, too, husband." She kissed his lips softly.

"Oh, you've done it now, Babe." He drew her closer, squeezing her. "I can't wait to get you alone. All fire and passion's gonna set the room aglow tonight."

"Sonny, we've got guest," She said, blushing. "

31

They're going to hear you."

"Yeah! Maybe they'll go home early." He laughed and started dancing her around the patio. After everyone had left, Sonny made good his promise to Dolores and made love until the wee hours of the morning.

Two weeks into their honeymoon, Dolores and Sonny found themselves babysitting.

"Michelle, your mama and I are still celebrating." He laughed and twirled Dolores around the room. "We have plans."

"Please, Daddy, it's our maid's night off. It's only for four hours."

"Ok, sure, but don't forget, you owe us one.

"You got it." Michelle smiled and headed for the door. "Eugene and I will be back early."

"Make sure it's early. I got plans for your mama tonight. He winked at Dolores and shook his body.

LOVE, PASSION AND HATE

A Faithful choice 2

CHAPTER 4

It was one week before Christmas. Dolores and
Sonny gathered the family to help decorate the
Christmas tree and to sample the eggnog that Mama
Kate was famous for preparing. Dolores had tried to
mix the eggnog according to the recipe. She dipped the
ladle in the mix and brought it to her lips. "Hmm. Not
quite. A little more nutmeg should do the trick."

James was the last to come home. He worked
late at the mill.

"Sit here, James. I saved this space for you."
Michelle moved over to make room and brought her
arm around his back to welcome her baby brother.

"Pass the eggnog, James," Dolores commanded
and set the punch cups on the coffee table.

"This family is complete except for Christy and
Eugene," Sonny said. "Where are they?"

"Christy is doing a great job running the fashion
house in New York." Dolores shook her head. "She'll
be here for Christmas."

When they had eaten and finished all of the
eggnog, Eugene opened the door and Michelle rushed
into his arms. "I'm going to have that talk with Martin."
He put his arms around her and kissed her. "I'll be

home early everyday with you and the children."

This brought a smile to Michelle's face and she hugged him tightly. "Oh, darling, you've made my night."

"I'm taking the twins shopping tomorrow. Want to come along?"

"No. I'll stay and fix your favorite dinner."

Michelle and Eugene took the children home. The next day, Eugene and the children shopped most of the day and returned when Michelle was setting the dinner table.

"Dinner will be short. I gave Valerie and Vilene a big lunch."

No worries. I'll put them to bed and we can spend time together."

Eugene had undressed, gotten into his robe and sat reading in the den. When she saw him, she hurried to the bathroom, undressed, got into her black silk lingerie and returned.

Eugene swept her into his arms and kissed her tenderly. "You're wonderful."

Michelle pressed herself against him and moaned in delight. "I love you, Eugene."

He picked her up in his arms, took her to their bedroom and reached for the scented oil on the night stand. He poured the oil into his hand, rubbed his hands together

and massaged it into her soft flesh. "Are you ready for

me?" He whispered in her ear.

"Yes, yes, Eugene."

They lay in each others arms for hours until they got up and showered together before going to sleep. They slept late the next morning until Dolores phoned.

"Don't tell me y'all still in bed. What happened over there last night? We've got Christmas gifts to wrap."

"Eugene and I had a private dinner," She answered, her voice silky and sensual.

"Get your butts out of bed and get over here," Dolores demanded. "It's Christmas Eve."

"We'll be over in an hour." She replaced the phone and kissed Eugene on the lips to awaken him. "Morning, darling. We've been summoned by the great matriarch for Christmas Eve."

Later that day, everyone sat around the Christmas tree, opening one present and exchanging story from past holidays. Sonny gathered the children and recited the Christmas Story. The children learned why Christmas was the family's favorite holiday.

THERESA GRANT

Christy had arrived earlier that morning and though it was Christmas Eve, Dolores was still a business woman. She and Christy talked a lot about the business. Velasco's had grown stronger and solvent. Dolores made more money that had already rendered her financially secure for the rest of her life and her children's life.

Dolores prepared their traditional party for family and friends. Soon the small number of guest started arriving.

Sonny greeted them, "Andre, my man. Brigit, you sexy thing, come here." He gave her a kiss on the cheek. Martin and his wife, Carissa, came through the door and he shook their hands.

Dolores hired Bob James and his trio and flew them in to play for the party.

"Everyone is in the Christmas spirit," Michelle said, observing the guest. "What are James and Christy doing in the corner?"

"They're discussing why Christy isn't pregnant," Dolores said, with sympathy in her voice. "They've tried for months with no luck."

Michelle wondered over to Christy when James left to get a drink. She put her arms around her in a sisterly fashion. "Ok, tell me all about your problem."
"I want a baby," Christy answered, her voice sounding awkward.

LOVE, PASSION AND HATE

A Faithful Choice 2

"What did the doctor say?"

"There's no reason, medically, why I can't." She sighed with exasperation.

James returned with the drinks and overheard their conversation. "Maybe I should have an examination." He said, joking.

Christy's smile broadened in approval and her mood became buoyant. She took him at his word. "Make an appointment tomorrow."

He was caught off guard by her sudden challenge of his manhood. Surly nothing could be wrong with him. He didn't want to argue and he promised, "I'll call the doc, tomorrow.

Sonny noticed that Christy and James weren't mingling. He came over and pulled Christy into his arms. "I've been searching for you, beautiful. Let's shake a leg."

Dolores took a seat by Carissa and inquired in a friendly manner, "How's everything?"

Misfortune had etched Carissa's composure and dignity. It showed on her face and she answered defensively, "Do you really want to know?"

Dolores' friendly smile faded. "I asked, didn't

I?"

She admitted with a cold edge of bitterness, "Marriage to Martin these days isn't easy."

"Whose fault is that, Carissa?" Her voice was harsh and raw.

Carissa came back at her. "Things could've been different if you'd loaned Martin the money." Those words made her want to die inside.

Her contemptuous tone sparked Dolores' anger and her voice was cold and exact. "I don't feel guilty. Martin's a grown man and he knew what he was doing."

"You've gotten hateful, Dolores." Hot fury flamed through her with a tremor in her voice. "I'm just trying to find my place in the sun."

"Well, you'd better do it yourself," She advised. "Don't depend on your man to fill all your hopes and dreams." Dolores got up to talk with her other guest, leaving Carissa alone.

Around midnight, everyone was tired, and after Sonny and Dolores had wished everyone a Merry Christmas and said goodbye, Dolores lingered in the party room and thought about her conversation with Carissa. "I just don't understand women who have no ambition."

"You must remember, everyone is not a

LOVE, PASSION AND HATE

A Faithful Choice 2

Dolores," Sonny said and kissed her. "Let's go to bed, I got something for you."

LOVE, PASSION AND HATE

A Faithful Choice 2

James relented after Christy reminded him of his appointment with the urologist. He had his test and was waiting for Doctor Roche. He entered and gave James the results. James's lips parted in shock. Then his jaw clenched, his eyes narrowed and he held his mouth taught before he cried out, "couldn't there be some mistake?"

"The test is conclusive," He handed him the report.

James staggered out of the doctor's office like a man given an anesthetic and was just coming around. He headed for the Rive Gauche and got drunk. It was two o'clock in the morning when he got home.

Christy met him at the door. "James? I've waited for you, sick with worry, going out of my mind and thinking all sorts of things." She shook her fist at him. "Where were you?"

"I'm sterile, Christy." He drew a sharp breath. "I'll never get you pregnant." He slumped to his knees, and tears fell down his cheeks.

A new anguish seared her heart. His words twisted and turned inside of her. Swallowing the sobs that rose in her throat, she gazed at him, stunned and sickened, and she repeated what he'd said, "You're

THERESA GRANT

sterile?" She slowly sat on the floor beside him.

He bowed his head, thrust his trembling hands forward and covered his face. He gave vent to the agony of his lost. "I'm sorry, Christy."

She stopped, long enough, to gather her composure and she saw the agonizing expression on his face. She wanted to relieve him of his pain. "We can adopt, darling. Hundreds of babies are waiting for parents like us."

"It won't be the same." He groped his chest, trying to ease the agony. "It won't be ours."

She put her arms around him. "Don't torture yourself for something that's not your fault."

"You'll never experience the fulfillment of being pregnant." He buried his face in her bosom.

"Don't do this to yourself, honey." She held him and placed her head to his head. "It's all right." She guided him to the bedroom, helped him get into his pajamas, into bed, and pulled the sheet and comforter over him before she got in next to him with her arm around him.

It was noon and they were still in bed. Christy heard the phone ringing but ignored it. The pain of seeing James in his state, last evening, and the report that he was sterile, still tore at her heart. Just thinking of it shattered her. When James turned over and answered the phone, she didn't move.

"I'm sorry about last night, Mom," his voice sounded tender, almost a murmur. "Dinner? I don't think we can make it for dinner."

How she could think of food at this time thought Christy, listening to James talking to Dolores, made her nauseous. Eating was the last thing on her mind.

"Maybe some other time, Mom," He said, apologetically. "Love you, too. Bye." He leaned over, moved the pillow, covering Christy's face, kissed her cheek and got out of bed to open the draperies.

The sunlight was too bright and she couldn't open her eyes. When she did, she gazed into his eyes, smiled, and said, "Morning, honey."

"I'm sorry about last night." He took her in his arms.

She rested her head against his chest, enjoying the warmth and comfort. "Together, we can get through this."

"He hesitated, measuring her for a moment, before he asked, "Does this mean you're not disappointed in me?"

A warning voice whispered in her head, choose your words carefully. He's in a delicate state. She swallowed hard, trying to manage a believable answer. "Course not. I love you. I'm happy with the two of us."

His gaze traveled over her face and searched her eyes. "If you're serious about adoption, I have a client with a pregnant teenager who is going to give her baby up next month."

Her heart jolted and her pulse pounded. A tingle started in the pit of her stomach. It was time to make good what she had said to him earlier. "Let's go for the adoption."

After lunch, James went to work and called his clients to discuss an adoption. He was in a better frame of mind

Christy got dressed to go to Dolores' chateau. If she and James were going to adopt, she had better let the family know. When she got there, everyone was in the kitchen. She blurted, "James and I are going to adopt a baby." She waited for their response, searching each one's eyes, hoping that they would be happy for her and James.

Michelle was skeptical. "Is this alright with you?"

"I'm delighted," She answered, annoyance hovering in her eyes. "Why do you ask?"

"Obviously, this girl is irresponsible, that's apparent by her pregnancy."

"So? What's that got to do with anything? I want

her baby."

"Can she be trusted to keep her word and give the child to you?"

Christy gave her a hard stare, wondering if she thought she and James were stupid. "Your brother is an excellent lawyer. He's handling the adoption and I trust his judgment."

Dolores frowned, then pinned Michelle with a knowing look and motioned for her to follow her outside the room. "My goodness, Michelle, what're you trying to do?"

"What?" She acted as if nothing had happened. "I'm trying to help."

"Why're you trying to spoil it for her?" Dolores whispered harshly and gave her a little shake.

"I wasn't. I just wanted her to know that they could be scammed."

"Dolores drew back with great firmness. "They got their minds set and nothing is going to change. Leave her alone."

"Gee. Ok. I was concerned. Maybe this is right for them."

They returned to the room and Michelle apologized. "I'm sorry, Christy. I didn't mean to sound critical."

"Forget it," She said and laughed in a deep jovial way. "I'm going to need all the help I can get and I'm depending on you all."

"Let's throw a party; a baby shower." Michelle put her arms around Christy's shoulder and hugged her.

Christy opened her mouth. No sound came out until she took a quick breath and wiped her tears. Then her face flushed with happiness and her brown eyes widened. "That would make it real for me."

"That's a great idea," Dolores said and hugged them both. "When's the baby due?"

Next month." Her spirit had heightened in a matter of seconds and she was overflowing with joy.

"We'd better get started." Michelle spent all week shopping for Christy's baby shower. Three days later, she was decorating Christy's family room in green and yellow. There were green and yellow balloons hanging from the ceiling with ribbons to match. A twenty-four inch stark, wearing a black top hat and carrying a baby doll in a diaper, was the centerpiece on a table decorated with green and yellow napkins, forks and spoons and a large sheet cake covered with white icing, green leaves and yellow roses.

A guest list of fifty noisy ladies, all of whom

were mothers, started arriving with gifts for the baby.

Michelle and Dolores served the food. They chatted, ate, drank and told stories about their labor pains, deliveries and babies. No one mentioned that Christy was adopting. They all acted as if she were having the baby.

Michelle took charge of the conversation and thought it time to stick to the order of how she had planned the party. "Ok, everyone, I want you to place a name in this paper bag." She handed the bag to Dolores to pass along. "We're going to help Christy choose a name for her babies."

"Names for a boy and a girl should be placed in the bag," Dolores said, collecting the names then shaking the bag. She handed it to Christy. "Draw a name, little mother."

Christy giggled with anticipation, drew one name and read it aloud, "Paula."

"That's a pretty name," Dolores said. "Draw another."

Christy drew a name and said, "Paul."

Everyone laughed and Christy's smile broadened in approval. "Those are great names for twins." Her heart sang with delight. She was blissfully happy, fully alive because, after today, she was going to be a mother.

Michelle gazed at Christy and glorified briefly,

"I shared in your moment of joy." Then she emptied the bag and made another request. "I want everyone to write a birth date and place it in the bag.

Christy drew a date from the bag when it was passed to her. "October 17th. That's close."

"Darn close," Michelle said, gathering the gifts and placing them beside Christy. "Let's see what little Paul or Paula will wear."

Christy opened a gift. "Aw! Oh! A beautiful woolen blanket. Thank you." She held it up for everyone to see. "I love pink."

"Let's see what else you've gotten." Dolores took the blanket, folded it and carefully put it back in its box.

"A blue blanket," Christy said. "This must be a sign." She opened the next gift and the next, and she had booties, christening gowns, diapers, bottles, towels, wash cloths and sheets. "With all of this, I won't have to shop for months." She stood and put her arms around Michelle and Dolores. Her face was flushed, her eyes bright, though watery from tears, and her smile wide. "Thank you guys for being my family and supporting me in this adoption."

"Our family may be dramatic, at times, but

we're always here for each other," Dolores assured her, holding her tightly. "You're part of us and the babies will be too."

After they'd eaten their fill and drank the last glass of punch, the guest went home.

The last day in October, Christy and James got a call from the hospital. They were the proud parents of twins. Christy could hardly contain herself as James drove to the hospital. "Can't you go any faster?"

"Not without exceeding the speed limit," James answered and laughed. "We're making good time. Here's Boulevard Victor Hugo."

When James pulled into the parking lot at the American Hospital of Paris, Christy rushed out of the car as James turned the ignition off. They hurried inside. Belinda, his client's daughter, had spontaneously given birth to a girl and a boy. The nurse brought the babies to Christy and put them in her arms. She cradled them, one in each arm. Her face was tender with a mother's love.

James, completely absorbed with the scene of Christy holding the babies, exhaled a long sigh of contentment. "I should've brought my camera. "What should we name them?"

"Let's call them Paul and Paula," She answered, gazing at them with tenderness.

LOVE, PASSION AND HATE

A Faithful Choice 2

CHAPTER 6

Martin had started drinking heavily. He was coming to work late and sleeping on the job. Eugene called him into his office. "You can't continue this behavior. It's bad for the company."

Martin rubbed his eyes. "I must've dosed off." He straightened his tie and brushed his hair back with his hands. "I couldn't have been asleep for more than an hour."

Eugene looked at him with disgust. "No one sleeps on the job. There's too much to do around here. The new fabrics will arrive today."

"Hey, I'm ready, for you, for them. You don't have to tell me what to do." His eyes, bloodshot, flat and hard, gazed at Eugene with hatred. "This was my company. I ran it before your in-laws stole it. You two-timing bastard."

"Let's not rehash old news, Martin, you know why that happened." He stood there looking at him as though he felt sorry for him. He was composed even in this difficult situation.

He didn't answer and he bald his fist to strike him, to make him feel the pain that his family had inflicted upon him. "Thieves," He shouted, jumped on Eugene and gripped his neck.

Struggling free, his brown eyes blazing, he

48

threw him aside. "Go home, Martin. I can't take this any longer." His violence took him by surprise. In all the years he'd known him, he never expected him to act in such a manner.

Again, anger singed the corners of his mouth, and he tried to take a swing at Eugene. He fell when Eugene ducked. "You can go to hell, Eugene. I don't want to work with you."

"Think of what you're saying," Eugene warned. "You're too old to start over."

Martin pushed him aside and staggered out of the office. He headed for the assembly line and called the employees. "The Brown's and the Glauerts' now own this mill. I was forced to give it over. No. I should say they stole it from me." He staggered about spitting out his venom to everyone. "I'm ruined. I'm poor."

Everyone began talking among themselves. They appeared worried as Martin continued, and a hush fell over the room.

"I want to thank you good men and women for your loyalty to me and my Father."

Some of the men, who had worked at the mill when Martin's father died and when he took over, put their arms around him and wept.

Martin went home and sat on the sofa. He sat for hours until Carissa came home.

"Martin, it's early." She stared at him with a
49

puzzling look. "What happened at the mill?"

He whirled and stared at her with contempt and quick anger rose in his eyes. "What does it look like, woman? Want me to draw you a picture?"

Her quiet voice held an undertone of indignation. "I simply asked you a question. No need to be nasty." She stood there looking down on him. "What's wrong?"

His voice was cold. "I've lost my job, the mill, everything. What else do you want to know?" He waved her away. "Leave me alone."

She paled suddenly, her breath burned in her throat and she massaged her temples. "After having so much, how are we going to get use to having nothing?" She put her head in her hands and wept. "Oh, your news has given me a horrid headache."

He put his arms around her and tried to calm her. "I'm going to look for a job tomorrow."

"A job?" She pulled away from him. "I shutter inwardly at the thought. You've never done anything except run the mill." She couldn't believe this man.

"I have a degree in business." His voice sounded resolute as he tried to assure her. "I can find something."

"Sell my jewelry and furs. They should bring us a few thousand." She felt a wretchedness she'd never felt before.

"You have no faith in me." His face flushed with humiliation and anger. "You're worse than Eugene. My own wife thinks I'm a loser."

"Please, Martin, I'm sixty-two and you're sixty-five. We're older now. Who's going to hire you at your age?" She tossed her graying hair over her shoulders.

"You'll see." He shook his fist at her. "You're going to eat those words." He rushed out of the den and went to one of the guest rooms, where he slept, without saying goodnight to her.

The next morning, Martin went out early. He had gone to all types of professional businesses. Then he tried all the textile mills within a fifty-mile radius, before returning home.

He sat on the sofa next to Carissa, wiped the sweat from his brow and removed his shoes. "I walked till my buns ached and I still don't have a job," He admitted with a deep sense of shame. He refused to meet her eyes as she stared at him.

Her thoughts were racing dangerously but she had to tell him. "Ask Eugene for your job. It'll be hard but what else can you do?"

His pride had been seriously bruised by her suggestion. Alarm and anger rippled along his spine. He shook his head vehemently, grabbed her by her wrist

51

and shook her. "Do you know what you're asking me to do? I'm a Fodor and we don't beg. Crazy bitch."

She gasped. Fear, stark and vivid, clutched her soul and she clamored to escape his disturbing presence. It was hours before she came out of her bedroom. She looked about to see where he was and wondered into the den. She dreaded another confrontation.

He gazed at her as tears rolled down his cheeks. "I put my hands on you and I'm sorry. I've never done that before and I promise never to do it again." He held her heart-shaped face in his hands and kissed her lips softly. "Please, forgive me."

"I'm sorry, too." She sat beside him, her slender, long fingers tensed in her lap. "I shouldn't have suggested you humble yourself before those selfish, hateful people."

"It'll be hard but we'll survive. Petunia, Felton and the other servants have to go."

"Not Petunia," She said nervously and bit her lip. "What will I do without a maid?"

"Again, he was a volcano on the verge of erupting. "You know I'd keep her if I could.

You've got to give up something. It's going to

be you, Steven and me."

She clenched her hands until her nails almost punctured her palms. "We forgot about our son. How is he going to finish school?" She became fearful again.

The tense lines in his face relaxed. "His money is in trust. He'll come out of this fine."

The tension between them began to melt and they found themselves in each other arms. "It's comforting to know that Steven will be his own man when he finishes college," She said.

"Yes, those bastards won't be able to ruin his life. Let's go and give our servants the bad news."

"I can't. My stomach is churning with anxiety and frustration. You'll have to tell them." She hurried from the room and pressed her ear to the wall to hear them talking. She knew this was cowardly, but she didn't want Petunia to see her crying.

Martin called Petunia and Felton. He took Petunia in the den while Felton waited in the family room. He cleared his throat and began, in a strained voice, "You've been with me since Steven was a baby. I love you but I can't keep you here."

Petunia let out a soft scream that echoed throughout the halls of the mansion. It sounded like a baby lion that had been separated from its mother. Then she composed herself and asked, "Why Mr. Martin?

What did I do?"

Carissa came out of the room and stood near the door. She saw tears staining Petunia's nut brown cheeks. Martin went to Petunia and put his arms around her. "It's not you. I've lost everything Father left me."

"I'm sorry about your misfortune, Mr. Martin." She took a moment to wipe her tears on her apron. "Cachlinque!"

"Yes, that stinks. I know it's a shock to you and I don't know what to say except I'm sorry."

"If that's the way it is, I'd better gather my things." She headed for her room.

"Don't rush. A week will be okay. It'll take that long to get your references ready."

Petunia left the room crying softly and Martin called Felton to talk to him. "You're a good chauffeur. I hate losing you."

"I too, Monsieur," He said, giving him the traditional French hug. I've loved working here. Bonne chance." They hugged and Felton sadly went his way.

"Good luck to you too." After Felton left, Martin called the gardener, the chef and the butler to give them their last pay check.

Two weeks later, Carissa searched through her closet for something to wear. "Look at these old wrinkled dresses." She missed Petunia pressing and laying her clothes out for her. "It's hard without servants. I've worn this same old dress three times already." She sighed and held the dress in front of her. "What will I wear if the crowd invites us to a party?"

Martin retained his affability but there was a distinct hardening of his eyes when he gritted his teeth and said, "No one's invited us since I lost the mill." He yelled at her. "Do you understand what I'm saying?"

Restless and irritated by his mocking tone, she conveyed her feelings. "It's boring here. I'm going to get a job."

She set him on edge. He jumped out of his seat. "I can't stand this any longer. Haven't I been humiliated enough?" He shook his fist at her. "You want to top it off by showing me you can get a job and I can't."

Again the tears were rolling down her cheeks. "Don't you get hysterical with me." She placed her hands on her hips. "I wasn't the one who got us into this mess."

"Throw it in my face, why don't you. Okay, it was my fault. I don't deny it, but do you have to rub it in?"

Suddenly weak and vulnerable in the face of his anger, she became furious with herself. Why should she give him the satisfaction of upsetting her? This could

last all day. She stared at him calmly and stated, "Let's not take our misery out on each other. If it'll make you happy, I'll find something to distract me." Then she thought of another solution. "Maybe I'll visit Steven in America."

Martin stared at her and shook his head. "He's an exchange student. Those people don't need you there meddling." When will this woman learn?

It was pointless to argue and she simply batted her eyes at him and said, "We'll see what Steven thinks. I bet he'd be glad to see his mother."

Martin had finished breakfast when he got a call from one of the offices he visited while searching for a job. "Yes, I can be there at 9 o'clock. See you then." He put the phone back on the kitchen counter and slapped his hands together. "We may be back in business, not a business of my own but I'll earn a salary. We can eat everyday and live in this house."

"What kind of job?" She wrinkled her nose and stared at him, lazily appraising his demeanor.

"He's a newcomer. Asia Roxbury is his name. He owns the finest house of fabrics along the Rue Saint-Florentin."

"He's not one of us but see him anyway," She urged. "Assuming that you're dealing with a reputable firm, insist on a high salary."

Martin went to see Asia. A short, dark secretary, not particularly pretty but supremely attractively dressed, guarded the entrance to his office. "May I help you?" She smiled at him with a half-smile.

"I'm Martin Fodor. I have an appointment with Mr. Roxbury." He started wringing his hands while she buzzed Roxbury and paced back and forth nervously when he hadn't answered. Could it be that he has changed his mind? His buzzer rang six times before he heard him say,

"Yes, Kim," he drawled in a New York accent.

"Mr. Fodor is here." She opened the door to his office.

Roxbury greeted him with a handshake. "Have a seat." He got right to the point. "I've heard about your expertise with fabrics. I want you to train my brother."

Martin felt as if a hand had closed around his throat as he tried to breathe. He started trembling. Then the muscles of his forearm hardened beneath the sleeve of his shirt. This couldn't happen to him again. He stared at Roxbury. "Didn't you advertise for a partner?"

"No. A mistake in printing," he said, waving his

57

cigar nonchalantly. "My brother is my partner or will be."

"I'm not a teacher, Mr. Roxbury." His cool, aloof manner irked him. "I'm afraid I've come to the wrong place."

"Ok, then, I had you pegged wrong. My secretary will show you out."

When Martin got home, Carissa was dressing to go out. Her whole face spread in a smile. She was eager and alive with affection and delight. "Martin, darling, Elvira and Daniel Larousse have invited us to dinner."

"I can't go tonight, Carissa." Depression settled in over him and he didn't want to hear any of her complaints. "I'm not feeling well."

She noted his set face, his clamped mouth and fixed eyes. "What happened with Roxbury?"

"Roxbury's brother is taking over. He wanted me to train him. I'll look for a job tomorrow."

"Aren't you being premature?" What more could go wrong in her life?

"Not at all. He wants to keep the business in the family. He's showing good sense. I should've done the same."

"But you didn't," She said boldly meeting his eyes, defiance in her tone as well as a subtle challenge. "Now you've got to find a job, any job. We need money."

A swift shadow of anger swept across his face and he yelled at her. "I don't need you to tell me my business. I'll get another job."

"Then come with me. Talk with Daniel. He may have something for you."

"Okay. It's better than sitting around feeling sorry for me."

At dinner, Elvira and Clarissa chatted about the ladies of the country club while Martin and Daniel talked politics.

"Inflation is rising," Daniel commented. "I like the president's economic plan."

"Some are saying it's all for his political gain," Martin replied.

"Poppycock! Thing will get better. He'll keep this country moving."

"Of course," Martin agreed. "My sentiments exactly."

"How's it going with you and Roxbury?"

"I'm glad you asked. I turned him down."

"I must go to Spain . . . straighten a few things out," Daniel said. "Take over the mill for me. I'll see what I can do when I return."

Martin's face lit with a smile. I'll start straight away." Now, he had to think of a way to get Carissa to agree, and it wasn't going to be easy.

As the evening ended at the party and Martin was driving home, he gave a sigh of relief. "It's going to be better working with Daniel. Though, I still don't like working for someone else, I'm glad I won't have to take orders from some young clod."

"No. We couldn't have that," Carissa said and kissed his cheek. "It's nice you'll be Daniel's assistant." The anguish in his eyes was so great that she didn't have the heart to argue with him.

CHAPTER 7

It was ten o'clock, the family usual time for Saturday breakfast. Michelle, Sherrie, Grace and Eugene Jr. entered the kitchen, while Eugene parked the car. "Morning, Grand-mamma!" Sherrie said and kissed Dolores. "Hmm, pancakes and sausage, American dishes."

"Hey! The gangs' all here." Christy said, bounding into the dining room. "Grace, give your aunt a good morning kiss. Grace went around the table and Christy bent down to receive her kiss. "Our little girl is getting chubby, eating this fattening food."

"Listen to who's talking," Michelle whispered to Dolores.

Christy pursed her lips. "I heard that, and I have you know I've lost weight."

"When?" Michelle asked and hunched Dolores.

"I lost three pounds last week, Missy, and don't tell me it doesn't show."

Dolores laughed and Michelle winked at her.

Christy paid no attention and began talking to Grace. "What would you like to do today?"

Grace placed a chubby little finger on her rosy, fat cheek and answered, "I want a Easter Bunny and chocolate egg."

"That's right!" Christy noted and tickled Grace's chin. Easter is next Sunday. I'll need to shop for Paula and Paul." They got in the car and drove to Velasco's.

Grace and Christy went to the candy department. Michelle stood by the counter eating chocolates from Belgium. She frowned when she saw them. "What took you so long? My feet are crying for some comfort." She limped about, holding onto the counters as she moved in pain.

Christy gazed at her feet. "I told you about wearing shoes too small for your feet."

Michelle put her hand on the counter to steady herself. "I'm wearing my correct size," She said in a perturbed tone. "Just go get the car."

Christy left and drove the car back to Velasco's entrance and Michelle limped to the car and got in the back seat. No one said anything on the way home. When she parked the car in the garage, Michelle walked in her bare feet to the kitchen.

Dolores had set the table and everyone sat down to dinner. "Pass those potatoes this way," Dolores said. "Michelle, why aren't you eating?"

"Must be all of that candy she ate," Christy said

and laughed.

"You've been on my case all day." Michelle's voice broke and she became angry. "What's your problem?"

"Let's finish this meal," Dolores commanded. "No need to get angry with each other. It's near time for the Friday night basketball game."

Sherrie arose from the table. "I can't watch. Got a date." She excused herself and went upstairs.

Christy was watching the chocolates and choosing her pick of the pieces.

"Girl! You don't need candy." Michelle said. "Your hips are bulging out of that dress."

"Thanks a lot," Christy waved her away and rolled her eyes at her.

"Well, do what you want. I'm taking Grace back to the store. I should've gotten her Easter dress while we were at Velasco's."

"I'm coming along," Sherrie said. "I need something to wear tonight."

They arrived at Velasco's and Sherrie started searching among the better dresses. She found a sleek, black silk dress with a slightly low cut neckline and carried it into the dressing room. She came out to view herself in the mirror. The dress was low cut in front, showing all of her breast, except her nipples, and tight fitting at the waist and hips. The shade of blue matched her caramel skin.

"Where are you planning to go in that dress?" Michelle asked. "What's the occasion?"

"My elusive boss, Mr. Link Barstow, is taking me out tonight."

"Wait a darn minute. He hasn't tried anything with you has he?"

"No, Mom. It's nothing like that now, but one day, he's going to be mine."

"Get your head out of sex games."

"He's lit a fire in my heart, Mom. He asked me to go to the Pocono Mountains for a week." She danced and pranced before the mirror and admired her reflection. "It looks sexy."

"No. It could lead to dangerous consequences."

"I'm hoping it will," She said and laughed. "I'll have to go to confession when I get back."

"Girl, you'd better behave yourself."

"Don't worry. I'm careful. Just making money, working for him until I finish school."

An hour later, after they'd returned from shopping, Link rang the doorbell. He stood in the doorway straight and tall, dressed in a gray pinstripe suit, blue shirt and tie, and gray fedora. He removed his hat, revealing jet black, curly hair neatly cut and shaped near the ears and nape of his neck. He came inside and stood near the television. "Who's playing?"

LOVE, PASSION AND HATE

A Faithful Choice 2

"Boston and New York," Michelle answered.

Before Link could get interested in the game, Sherrie entered the room and his eyes flashed. He gazed at her heart shaped face. She'd cut her hair short in a style that was becoming. His eyes traveled the length of her and he took her hand. "We don't want to be late." He led her out to his black Mercedes.

Everyone rushed to the window and watched them get into his car. When he helped her into his car, he almost slammed the door on his hand and Michelle laughed and said, "I think I'm going to get a son-in-law, but after she finishes college."

The next morning, Michelle, the twins, Grace and Dolores were eating breakfast when Sherrie entered the dining room. She slumped at the table and blew hard.

"Those late hour dates will tell on you every time," Michelle reminded her. "How was your date with Mr. Bright eyes?" She laughed and touched Dolores' shoulder.

"Must've been some night," Dolores said. "Hope you're still positive."

"We had dinner and drinks at his apartment. It was an evening made in heaven."

"Does that mean you're going to see him

again? Walk in the spirit not in the flesh," Michelle commanded. "You'd better think more on your lesson and God."

"Got it covered, Mom."

"Where's that husband of mine?" Dolores asked going to the window and peering out.

"Probably in the park with Paul, Paula and Grace," Michelle said. "He loves spending time with his grandchildren."

No sooner had she spoken when Sonny barreled through the kitchen door with the children. He caught his breath and sat down at the table. "Boy, we sure had fun."

"Feeling ok today, Daddy?" Michelle asked.

He gestured and boxed the air. "Like a young buck."

Dolores laughed and winked at Michelle. "He still thinks he's a young man, even in bed."

Sherrie missed the joke, looked puzzled and tried to steal a kiss from Paul and Paula.

They were finishing breakfast when the phone rang. Sherrie got to it first. "Hi, Link. Dinner?" She smiled, covered the telephone with her hand and whispered to Michelle, "I've got a plan."

LOVE, PASSION AND HATE

A Faithful Choice 2

"Play it smart," Christy advised. "Not too fast."

Sherrie spoke slowly into the phone, "Sorry, Link, I've got a date." There was a pause and she continued, "You know Oscar Price," practically singing his name. "Tomorrow? Let me look at my calendar."

"Don't say yes," Christy whispered to her.

Sherrie silenced her and continued talking. "If it's important, Oscar will understand." She let the phone fall slowly into its receiver and floated back to the table. "Link is taking me dancing tonight." She smiled and went up stairs to get ready.

After dinner, Dolores and Michelle went to the family room to look at television.

Michelle talked about Eugene and herself. "I don't know where it's all going to end with Eugene and me. We're so unhappy."

He's been overwhelmed by work," Dolores reminded her. "Try being more understanding."

"Daddy works hard. He's proud, yet he works as a mill hand," Michelle said.

"He didn't always work hard, nor was he proud," Dolores informed her. "When I first met him, he worked at the Mobile Recreation Center."

"I never knew he worked there."

"We both did, after I ran away from home.

"Mom, you were feisty"

"Had to be if I wanted to survive." Her thoughts floated back to the time she lived with Mama Kate and Jake, the son-of-a…"

"What else should I know about you and Daddy's life?" She laughed, wiggled her nose and sniffed. "Tell it all. I want to hear about your little escapades."

"Some things are better left unsaid. Let's just leave it at that. Be thankful that you have a hard working husband." She took her hands in hers. "Eugene's a good father and he loves you and the children."

It was tough for you, wasn't it Mom? You had James and me to care for making $10,000 a year." She looked at her with respect and was thankful for the closeness that they shared as mother and daughter.

"When you're young and in love, you get married and sometimes, it doesn't last, it takes great effort to keep it together." Her eyes started to well and she dried her eyes. "That's all behind us now. I'm a rich woman. I'm happy and you should be too."

"I know. I should count my blessings. I've got to get home." She gathered her things and kissed Dolores. "Thanks for helping me see the light."

"What are mothers for?" She gave her a kiss and

LOVE, PASSION AND HATE

A Faithful choice 2

a hug. "Go home to your husband."

Eugene came home early that evening carrying three gifts and a birthday cake with a big blue, iced number fifty in the center surrounded by the inscription, "Happy Birthday Michelle."

"You didn't forget."

"I've thought of nothing else all week."

One could hardly read anything in Eugene's handsome, seductive face, but this time he had shone a serene, look of love and caring. He took her hand, kissed it, reached into his pocket and withdrew a large, beautiful ruby ring surrounded by a circle of blue-white diamonds. "Happy birthday, darling." He slipped the ring on her finger.

Michelle, mesmerized, held the ring up to the light and planted kisses over his face. "I love it." This loving act of Eugene's relieved the anxieties that she felt over him being away from home.

He laughed and pulled her into his arms. "Like it?"

"Try taking it from me," She said, watching the diamonds sparkle. She took his hand. "C'mon. Let's eat. I've prepared baked red snapper-stuffed with crab meat, creole gumbo, corn muffins and pecan pie."

"Hmm, fit for a king."

69

THERESA GRANT

"It's for a king," She said. "You, darling."

Eugene smiled, kissed her and announced what he knew she wanted to hear. "I've decided to let the foreman run the mill for awhile. I discussed it with Sonny and he's agreed."

"Now you're talking, darling." She began setting the table with her favorite white linen and blue china. After dinner, she put Grace and the twins to bed so that they could be alone. They hadn't been alone since Grace was born, and she was making this night one he'd never forget. She slipped into a long black, silk lounger with a low v-cut neckline and t-straps. Happy with laughter, she peered at herself in the mirror, tilted her head and threw one shoulder forward. "Tonight's the night," She sang, sprayed her neck with Chanel 5 perfume and got in bed. "Eugene," She called. "I've got something for you."

Eugene, sitting in the den with a glass of Champagne in his hand, came into the bedroom, took one look at her, smiled happily and got in bed beside her. He felt as if his blood had turned to fire and caused every cell in his body to scream with desire.

The next morning, before Eugene got out of bed, Grace entered their room and climbed into bed with him and Michelle. Eugene kissed her and hugged her tightly. "Daddy's happy to see you."

Grace had been coloring pictures and she

70

handed one to Eugene for his approval.

"What do we have here?" He tickled her stomach and made her laugh. "Gee, you're better than some of the artists I've commissioned to work on the fabric at the mill. You're a natural born artist."

She laughed merrily as she put her coloring away

After eating breakfast, Eugene got ready for work.

"Will you be home to celebrate Grace's fourth birthday?" Michelle asked gazing at him.

"I meant what I said last evening. I'll be here."

"I've got to go to the bakery and order the cake." She said. "Maybe I can get Sherrie to pick it up after her classes."

"Whatever." He kissed her and gave Grace a hug and a kiss. "See you later."

Sherrie entered the dining room and poured a cup of coffee. "I have three exams today. I was up late studying."

"After class, can you get the cake from the bakery if I order it for Grace?"

"Oh, little Sister is four years old today?" She went around the table and kissed her. "Of course I can.

71

THERESA GRANT

I wouldn't miss eating cake and singing happy birthday."

"We're going to head over to Mom's for brunch. Bring the cake there." She dressed Grace, made sure that Valerie and Vilene were dressed and drove to Dolores' chateau.

Dolores was in the kitchen with Rosalie, the cook. Grace began trying to help. She loved puttering around in the Kitchen with Rosalie and watching while she prepared meals. As Rosalie began filling the serving dishes, Grace would set them on the dining room table.

That evening, after dinner, everyone sang happy birthday to Grace and Sherrie left to go to work.

Sherrie got to work as Link was arriving. He removed his hat, revealing a new style to his hair. His beard and sideburns had been trimmed shorter. She was in a daze as she gazed at him. She spoke and the sound of her voice was shrill. "Are you and Mr. Galloway meeting this evening?"

"Yes. We will be working on some briefs and I'll need you to take dictation."

It was eight o'clock when they finished. "I'm calling it a day," Mr. Galloway said, gathering his

LOVE, PASSION AND HATE

things.

"And you, Sherrie?" Link asked. "Would you care to have dinner with me?"

"I'd love to."

"Then let's go, lovely lady." He headed for Champs de Mars. "Want to try the Altitude 95 Restaurant on the first floor of the Eiffel Tower?"

"Whatever. They have great food. I don't mind."

That's what I like about you; you're so agreeable." He kissed her cheek.

They arrived, were seated and ordered from the menu. While they waited for the food, he whispered in her ear, "You are so beautiful."

She blushed and smiled into his eyes. His aura made her skin tingle. "You always know the right things to say to a girl."

"It's not hard when I'm with you." He gave her hand a squeeze. Do you like to ski?"

"I love it."

"I have a villa on the Riviera. Will you go with

73

THERESA GRANT

me this weekend?"

"Sounds like fun. I can have most of my work done for my classes and be ready to leave when you say."

After dining on grilled beef and vegetables, and drinking Burgundy, they had their fill and headed for home. "I'll call for you Friday evening," He said. "I have all of the necessary attire for skiing."

"Great! I'll be ready." They waved goodnight as she went inside the house.

That Friday, Sherrie could hardly contain herself. "I'm going skiing for the weekend with Link," She announced to everyone.

"Where is Mr. Money bags taking you?" Dolores asked.

"He has a villa on the Riviera."

"Oh, what elegance," Christy, teased her. "Remember, take it easy. Don't do anything foolish."

"She'd better not," Michelle said. "Remember what Pastor Lyles said in church."

"Come on, Mom. It's just skiing."

"Make sure that's all it is. Remember Pastor Lyle's class on "Love before Marriage."

74

LOVE, PASSION AND HATE

A Faithful Choice 2

When Link arrived, Sherrie hurried out to his car, threw her suitcase in the back and climbed inside next to him. He took the fastest route; the AutoRoute, which began at Porte d' Orleans. It started snowing before they arrived and by nightfall, it had snowed heavily. "This is good. By tomorrow, it will be nice for skiing."

"It's beautiful in here among the exotic vegetation." She sniffed the air. "Orange, eucalyptus, lemon, olive and pink laurel fills the air."

"It's quite enjoyable," he agreed.

"It's also cozy in this villa. I wouldn't care if we ever went outside." She moved closer to him. "Being snowed in with you is like ---oh-----just hold me in your arms and kiss me till I'm numb all over."

"Why, darling, have I that much of an effect on you?"

"More than you know, Link. I think I'm falling in love with you."

He took her in his arms and kissed her. Then eased his hold and began to undue his belt. He slowly unzipped his pants, took her in his arms and led her to the bed.

Her desire for him was strong, but she knew that she must get a hold of herself and she feared if he touched her again, she couldn't trust herself to resist

75

him. "Stop!" She cried.

He quickly released her. "I'm sorry. I thought you wanted me as much as I wanted you."

"It's got to be different with us; not like this and in here."

"When and where?"

"I need more time," She replied. "Let's get to know each other better."

"It's been nearly a year. How long does it take to make it with you? A decade?" He asked angrily.

"Please, don't be angry. We have to wait until the moment is right."

"Ump." He got his clothes in order. He had a disgusting look on his face. "Your room is down the hall." He took her things and set them inside for her and then went to his room.

It was a chilly night for both of them and the next day they got up, had breakfast and started for the slopes. They didn't talk much. Then Sherrie broke the silence. "I'm sorry about last night. I didn't mean to give you're the wrong impression."

"Let's just forget it and have fun."

"I'm all for good, clean fun," She said and smiled. She worried about the mistake she'd made in confessing her love for him. He seemed distant and she

wasn't having the time with him she'd expected. They both could hardly wait for Sunday and to head back to town.

That following week, Sherrie spent a lot of time in the office with Link. "Would you like me to stay again after work?"

"No. Go on home. I can handle it alone."

"You don't have to," She persisted. "I'm available."

"Thanks, but no."

She muttered under breath as she left, "Mr. Barstow doesn't want to be taken seriously. He just likes to have fun and leave it at that."

He didn't say anything and she left the building feeling dejected. She was falling in love with him and the problem was that he knew it.

One morning, Link announced that he was leaving the firm. "I want to branch out into my own office. I think now is the time." As he was gathering his things together for the move, Sherrie entered his office.

"Link, why are you leaving?"

"It's better that I do this now."

THERESA GRANT

"I'll come with you, if you ask me," She said with an astonished look on her face.

"No. It'll be better for both of us if we parted friends here."

"Just what're you afraid of."

"Afraid? Me?"

"Yes. Every time I try to get close you practically run away. What is it with you?"

"Okay. Since you've pressed the issue. I'm not ready to get involved, seriously, with anyone." He flailed his arms in air. "Maybe later. Not now."

After Link left, Sherrie was hurt. As much as she'd prayed that he felt about her as she felt about him, and that he was the man for her, she realized he definitely wasn't him. She left the firm and went to work for Mr. Billoway's law office. She continued to live at home with her parents. With the way the economy was going, she was living comfortably and cheaply. After all, where could she get such good home cooking like Mamma's and Grand- mammas? Being single and living at home had its advantages.

LOVE, PASSION AND HATE

A Faithful Choice 2

CHAPTER 8

Martin had worked three months for Daniel and was doing everything to make a good impression; including overtime and the extra work of others. It was going well until Daniel returned from Spain.

"How would you feel about working in Spain as manager? Daniel asked.

"I've got to discuss it with Carissa, but I'm sure she'll agree; I need something permanent." He knew this wasn't going to set well with her but he would have to try and reason with her.

"Let me know soon. Elvira wants me home."

Martin was excited. He could hardly wait to discuss it with Carissa. When he got home, he found her in the kitchen taking a roast from the oven. He came behind her, grabbed her in a bear hug and kissed her neck.

"Watch out!" she exclaimed, pushing him away. "I nearly dropped the dinner."

"Sorry, honey," he said grinning like a Cheshire Cat. "Guess what? Daniel offered me a permanent position in Spain."

She gasped and said, "You got to be kidding. I

love this house---this town. I won't leave."

"You won't have to," he assured her. "I can come home on weekends."

"Forget it!" she said, stomped her foot and slammed the roast on the table. "I object. You can't leave me alone here." His words rang in her ears as she wiped her eyes on her apron.

He tried reasoning with her, though he was getting frustrated. "I fought hard to keep this house for you and Steven," He said. "It's the only thing I've left to leave."

"It infuriates me when you're like this," She mused out loud. She was livid, overflowing with rage and had to get it out of her system.

"We must settle this, Carissa. Daniel expects an answer."

Her voice quivering, she yelled, "I know you've got to have a job but find one here. I won't stand for this."

"Where might that be?" He closed his eyes while waiting for her to answer.

She threw herself on the sofa, cried, got up, stood in front of him and pointed her finger close to his face. "I won't be alone here."

"Steven will be home soon. You won't be alone.

LOVE, PASSION AND HATE

A Faithful Choice 2

We've got to come to terms with this, Carissa."

"Okay, Martin, I understand you've got to have a job, but it's very disappointing that it's out of town." She turned around, sauntered out, and slammed the door behind her.

Later that evening, Martin called Daniel and began making arrangements to leave for Spain in three days. He felt as though he was suffocating as he talked to Daniel. "I'm going."

"It was a cold Friday morning when Martin left town. He was gone for all of the winter months before he came home. Carissa was happy to see him but angry with him. "Martin, did you have to stay away so long without so much as a call to let me know that you weren't coming home? I felt so alone here. You promised every weekend." She flashed her angry brown eyes at him.

"I know but there was so much to be done. I was bogged down in paper work, orders to be filled and late bills to be sent out." He was frustrated and tired. "I fell in bed, thereafter, to do the same every night."

"Couldn't you've made one call? Inquire after my health or if I had died?" She asked angrily. "I guess nice wives finish last, huh?"

"Don't be so dramatic, Carissa." He flung his hands in air. "I neglected to call. I'm sorry. I'm doing

81

my best. Don't you think I'd rather be here with you? So much for coming home to a loving wife." He's never seen her so spiteful.

"Let's not quarrel." She softened her tone. "We need to take advantage of these two days before you leave." She knew that she had said too much.

He pulled her to him. "It's been hell being away from you."

She pressed closer to him. "The nights were cold without you. I missed feeling your body next to mine." Her hand touched his face and she declared, "I don't want to get in the way of you doing your job."

"No worries. It's a piece of cake. Daniel isn't demanding. I know. What if I took you with me and we could return home on weekends?"

"Oh, Martin, that would solve a lot of my problems. You know how I love traveling and exploring new places." Her face lit with a bright smile and she felt happy and serene.

Martin took Carissa with him and, after that, when he went out of town, she went along.

She regretted everything that she had said. "I enjoy these trips and dining in delicate restaurants."

"I've noticed, but you love shopping more than

82

eating," He said and pinched her round dimpled cheeks.

There was no limit to what Carissa purchased. Martin gave her an allowance in the amount of $5,000.00 to buy whatever she wanted. He loved to see her dress. He purchased exquisite furs and jewelry to match whatever she'd bought. Daniel paid him well.

They were having a great time until Steven called. "Where are you two? I'm home."

"We'll be home on the weekend," Martin said. "Glad you're home, Son."

That weekend, Martin and Carissa came home. Steven met them at the door. "Mom." He kissed her and stroked her hair. "Happy to see you, Dad." He hugged Martin and helped with the bags. "Did you give Felton and Petunia the day off? Where is the help?"

"Long story, Steven. Your father lost the mill and he's got some crazy notion of getting back his fortune in Spain."

"How did he come to this?" He sat with a worried look on his face.

"Poor judgment, failed investments----you name it," She answered, letting him know how disappointed she was with him. It was time he knew the truth. "I found he'd been spending weekends at Long champs

Race Way; playing the horses and drinking heavily."

"Mom, please tell me it's not true." He wiped the moisture off of his face. "Why didn't you write to me? I would've come home."

"No. You must take care of yourself and your future, Steven. He didn't touch your trust fund." She sat with her arms around him. "He's working, for Daniel Larousse, as manager of the mill in Spain. Daniel's a good man. He'll help your father."

"Still, we've never been beholden to anyone. Grandfather was a proud man."

"And a good business man," She said. He blames the Glauerts and the Browns for his misfortune but he brought it on himself."

"What are you going to do, Mom? How are you making it?"

"Your father is making a great salary. I believe he'll recover and own his own mill some day."

"What can I do to help?"

"Encourage him. Help him to get back on track."

"I could put my money with his and build a new mill. I can't have this money, knowing that our family needs it."

Carissa's heart started pounding. The thought of

getting back into the upper echelon appealed to her. "Talk to him about it. You may be right. You know your father and I would do anything for you."

"And, I for you."

"Convince your father. He'll listen to you."

Martin returned to the sitting room and sat next to Steven. "What are you going to do, now that you've graduated from Harvard?

"I want to get our family's respect back. I'll give you my trust and we'll build a new mill."

Why did you have to tell him, Carissa?" He stared at her with an ache in his heart. "You're never going to let me deal with this, are you? I made a mistake and I'm paying for it but I can break out of this rut."

"There's no need for you to do it alone, Dad. I'm here now and, together, we can rebuild what Grand Father wanted for this family."

LOVE, PASSION AND HATE

A Faithful Choice 2

CHAPTER 9

It was a beautiful sunny day and Sherrie was playing tennis at the mansion of Eugene's longtime friend, Bruce Deplore. He'd invited her and Christy to his mansion, but a tennis game wasn't holding her interest, much to the dismay of Christy.

"Are you going to play with me or those men on the next court?" Christy asked.

"What men?" She pretended not to notice but wasn't fooling Christy.

"Oh, it's like that now? You could never lie and keep a straight face," Christy said.

Sherrie turned to see them watching her and laughed when one missed his ball.

The one wearing red tennis shorts swore to his partner, "Damn! This game is yours."

"That's one for me," his partner yelled and chuckled.

The looser threw his racket on the court and hopped over the net.

His partner laughed and called to him, "Where are you going, Steven? Don't be a sore loser."

"I've got to meet this beautiful diversion. See you tomorrow, Pierre."

Sherrie watched him as he came toward her smiling, and she whispered to Christy, "Oh, he's fine!"

"You could say that," Christy whispered, swinging her racket. "Not my type, though."

Course not, silly. He's mine." Steven came closer and she grew nervous. "My heart is doing flip flops and about to jump out of my chest. Look at that body, those muscles, and those ample juicy lips. He's a fox!"

"I'll admit he's got nice biceps," Christy said with an impatient shrug.

He was standing in front of her, gazing at her long wild raven curls and her peach colored skin, her tall, graceful figure dressed in white shorts and a t-shirt that revealed her tight, ample breast. "What's your name?"

"Sherrie Glauert." She sang and batted her eyes at him.

"You caused me to lose a game today, Sherrie." He continued scrutinizing her.

She flashed her big brown eyes at him and played little Miss innocent. "Moire?"

"Yes. You distracted me. Do you come here

often?"

"My first time." His deep bronzed face was drenched with sweat, but he was the handsomest man she'd ever seen. "If what you say is true, Mr---"

"Steven Fodor, Harvard graduate, business scholar and heir to one of the best fabric mills in Paris."

"Presumptuous and arrogant," She whispered through her teeth, but that didn't detour her, instead, she wondered what it would be like to bask in the warmth of his massive arms.

Down you impetuous girl, she thought and declared, "I can do nothing about your game."

"Have dinner with me tonight and I'll forgive you," He said, enjoying his little game of teasing her

Christy bumped her leg, motioning her to say no.

She paid her no attention, fished in her tennis bag for a pen and piece of paper, scribbled her address and handed it to him.

"See you tonight, Sherrie. Is seven o'clock ok?"

"Fine," She said, watching him walk away. "Oh, I think I'm in love."

"You just met the man. Temptation comes and it

can come strong."

"Haven't you heard of love at first sight? Really, Christy, where is your imagination?"

That evening, Sherrie had dressed and was waiting for Steven and so was every member of her family. She had asked Dolores to answer the door. Dolores was curious after Sherrie had raved about Steven. She gladly complied. When he knocked, Dolores opened the door.

Sherrie heard Steven's masculine voice, which to her sounded like someone playing a base horn. "Evening, Madam, I'm Steven Fodor."

"Mrs. Dolores Brown," She replied in her soft motherly voice. "Are you related to Martin Fodor?"

"Yes, Madame, he's my Father."

Dolores led him to the parlor and Sherrie hurried toward him. "Meet my Father and Mother, Eugene and Michelle Glauert, my Grand Father Sonny Brown and my sisters: Valerie, Vilene and Grace."

Steven bowed. "It's a pleasure, Sirs—ladies."
Michelle held her head and closed her eyes, took a deep breath and asked, "Did your Father mention the Glauert's?"

"Not that I can recall. Do you know my parents?"

"We were once partners," Eugene informed

89

A Faithful Choice 2

him.

"That's odd that he never mentioned you, but I was in school in America."

"Obviously, we have much in common," Sherrie said. "But it's getting late. Let's be on our way."

He took Sherrie's hand, helped her outside and into his car. "Move it, Kolas."

The chauffeur drove the black Aston Martin on the road south to Coulommiere, and then followed the N.34 Route. After an hours ride, they came through a winding drive that seemed to be a maze. Then suddenly the mansion came into view and Sherrie was impressed. Never had she seen such a graceful mansion, a magnificent edifice of the 14th and 17th centuries surrounded by two huge stone gods guarding the entrance to the gate and tall columns across the front of the chateau with six windows on each side and majestically sitting on a hill surrounded by acres of land with lush green foliage, carefully trimmed poplars and willow trees. They entered the chateau and he led her to the library that seemed to be patterned after the Louis XIV period. She wondered over to the fireplace that was large enough to step into and fingered the marble.

"Every stone imported from Italy," he said.

"She sighed and said, "Beautiful."

"Everything in here is very pure and very old; the paintings and tapestries." He said and took her hand. "We're eating in the dining room." He seated her at a French provincial dining table for twelve people. "My Mom and Dad will be dining with us."

His parents entered and took a seat at the dining table. Both scrutinized her for a moment without so much as a smile or a blink of the eye.

Steven made the introductions, "Sherrie Glauert, My Mom, Mrs. Carissa and Dad, Martin Fodor."

Carissa shook her hand but Martin did not, and began questioning Steven. "Did you visit the site for the mill?"

"Yes, Dad," he barely said, above a whisper.

"A man is nothing without his business. My life's blood and sweat was in my family's mill."

"So was Mom's," Steven said bitterly, remembering how she tried to keep the family strong and together.

Martin stared sadly at Steven. "I wasn't with her when she gave birth to you, but a man does what he's got to do," He said, sounding remorseful.

Steven narrowed his eyes and said, "You were

at the mill while she laid suffering."

"Everything would've been lost if I hadn't," He stared at him with a look of sorrow.

"It was lost anyway." Steven said and shook his head. "It was all in your hands."

"I've heard all of those arguments from your mother." He cast a mean stare at Sherrie. "Daniel gave me a chance to redeem myself."

"I've heard the story, Dad. He gave you a job."

"Can't say that for the scoundrels that stole our family's mill."

"Let's not rehash those ancient problems," Steven said. "We're thinking about the future."

"You don't know a thing about what happened." What could he do to make him understand? What does he know about what he went through?

"You've told the story a trillion times. Let's just enjoy the meal."

"I've lost my appetite." He rose from the table, threw his napkin aside and left the room.

"I'm sorry," his mother said and excused

herself. She looked back and half-smiled with tears in

"Pay no attention to Dad," Steven said, with a far away look in his eyes. "His first love is the mill, but not mine."

"Must be tuff filling your father's shoes. You've got a lot to live up to."

"I'm not Dad, never will be and don't want to be. My Grandfather was my idol."

He held a fire in his eyes that seemed a little frightening to Sherrie but, in spite of what she thought were his shortcomings, she wanted him.

He moved his chair closer to hers and stared into her eyes. He had a habit of starring a person right in the face, which you would never catch most parishes' doing. "Tell me about you."

She drew closer and answered, "I'm studying business and psychology at the university."

"Why those subject?"

"I expect to be involved in my family business and I want to prove my theory about what people have in common with tigers and lambs." She said. "It's all about survival. All humans are animals. We're here to kill or be killed, and survive."

"Where did you get that from?" He gazed at her and laughed.

LOVE, PASSION AND HATE

A Faithful Choice 2

"It's true. People are either tigers or lambs, nothing more, you eat or get eaten. I use to be a sheep; the food, and now I'm a tiger surviving in the jungle."

"That's bull."

"Don't get me wrong—I'm still a kind, caring person, but I'm now a cautious tiger looking out always for myself, protecting my family and the person inside of me."

He took her in his arms and held her. "Who hurt you? You were in a bad relationship, weren't you?"

She told him the story of Link and herself, how he tried to take advantage of her and mistook her love for weakness; a sheep. "Live like a tiger, act like a tiger. Trust me, it works."

"Your theory is interesting but a little scary," he said.

"When dealing with people, ask your self, 'what does this person want from me'? Nine times out of ten they're trying to help themselves and not you."

"Never have I met anyone like you. I have to admit you're interesting and I want to get to know you."

"And I you, but for now, it's been a great evening," She said. I've enjoyed everything, including the conversation."

He squeezed her waist and stared into her eyes. "There will be others better than tonight." He retrieved

the phone and rang for Kolas to bring the car around.

After their first date, Sherrie and Steven were partners on the tennis court and he visited her everyday after her classes. One afternoon, after a late class, she found him sitting on the university's steps. "How long have you been here?" She asked, beaming, when she saw him.

"A couple of hours. Want to go to a party?"

She rocked her head and pretended to give it some thought. It wouldn't be smart to appear eager. She won't make that mistake twice, though she wasn't about to refuse. "Sounds like a lot of fun but I can't be ready till seven."

"No matter. I'll wait, whatever the time."

This man is serious, she thought. He's a tiger, but courteous, respectful and caring. Be still my heart. She put her hand to her chest and felt her heart.

It was 7 o'clock when Kolas pulled up to her house and she came out wearing a black, silk dress, cut low to the waist, opened in back, high in front and sleeveless. The white pearl

necklace and earrings that Michelle had given her for

Christmas made the dress look even more elegant.

Steven looked at her and whistled. "You look beautiful."

They arrived at Pierre's party and entered a huge, old prestigious mansion filled with priceless antiques and fine European furniture. The elaborate entertainment room was decorated like a rooftop garden and ablaze with large, twinkling lights covering variously colored silk lanterns. It was the site of a private and intimate party.

Steven and Sherry mingled between the guests and danced a couple of times.

"We're the only singles here," Sherry noted.

"Except Pierre. But don't worry. I've planned to change our situation."

"Oh, listen to you, tiger, and how are you going to change our situation without asking me?"

"I was----tomorrow but now's a good time. Will you?"

"Will I what?" She wanted him to say the words.

"Marry me?"

"I'll think about it." She smiled up at him and

traced the line of his lips with her little finger.

He caught her finger between his lips, kissed it and said, "I want this marriage."

She was excited now, more than ever, but she drew back, gazed into his eyes and said, "I need more time."

"What's there to think about?" He asked, spinning her around in his arms. "We're like cake and ice cream, caviar and champagne."

"Enough already!" She said laughing. "I want a June wedding."

"Darling, you can have whatever it takes."

"I also want us to sign a prenuptial. I'll sign yours and you sign mine."

He gazed at her as if she'd lost her mind. "What's the big deal?"

"At some point I'm going to inherit a certain percentage of my Father's mill. You're going to inherit yours."

"So?" He gazed at her serious face. "What's your point?"

"My family won't leave me anything if they think it's going to be taken away."

He grew angry and snapped at her, "So, that's what you think of me?"

"It's reality, Steven. Remember what I said about the tiger and the lamb? It's not you, it's instinct only." She took his hand and tried to get him to understand. "My parents are doing what they have to. It's called survival."

He gazed at her and shook his head."

"Think about it and let me know," Sherrie said. "If you don't want to marry me, I'll understand."

"You're crazy, do you know that?"

"Talk it over with your parents. You'll see. I'm right."

When Sherrie finished her last year at the university, she and Steven were getting married. The Glauert family, not the Fodor's, were happy that evening. It was ten o'clock that Saturday morning when Sherrie marched down the isle wearing a white silk organza dress, bordered with laced rose petals, netted veil connected to a train that extended ten feet long, and white satin shoes with pearl bows near the toe. Yellow and white daisies, lily of the valley and baby's breath surrounded the bouquet that she carried.

Six bride's maids wore chartreuse dresses and wide brimmed satin hats to match. Grace, Paula, Vilene and Valerie, as flower girls, wore pink dresses with pink ribbons in their hair and threw pink roses from their natural straw baskets that were draped with pink ribbons.

The reception was held in Dolores' back yard

There were one hundred guest and a few were enquiring about the honeymoon plans, which was a well kept secret but not from Michelle. "Where're you taking my daughter?"

Steven silenced her with a finger to her lips, then whispered, "I have a summer home in the hills of Province above the Cote d' Azure."

"Mediterranean beaches, underwater wonderlands and magnificent views. Honeymoon time is a good time for that area," Michelle said. "Leave now. I'll give everyone your regards."

Sherrie kissed her, took Steven's hand and slipped quietly away. The moment they arrived at the summer home, Sherrie loved the peace and beauty of the calm, relaxed atmosphere.

"What a place! It's sheer heaven." She ran from one room to the next. "The view of the sea from the walk-in bay window is fascinating."

Steven was behind her laughing all the way until she came to the master bedroom. He pulled her down on the early English and canopied bed and took a moment to catch their second wind. "I love the way your eyes light up when you're happy," He said and began to unbutton her dress.

Sherrie blushed at the thought of undressing before him, for the first time, and she got up and hurried to the bathroom. She turned the handle of the gleaming brass faucet and watched, smiling, as the soft water flowed into the drop-in bowl, down against its delicate shell pattern. She removed her make-up, rinsed her face then slipped out of her dress and into her gown. Pausing for a moment, she opened the door and peered into the bedroom. Steven was waiting in bed for her and she slid in next to him. "I love you."

"I love you," he declared and kissed her.

The touch of his hand made her moan with pleasure and she awaited his next passionate move, as she opened her mouth and tasted his tongue as his lips closed over hers. Many hours of lovemaking had past and they lay in each others arms.

After two weeks on their honeymoon, Sherrie and Steven went home. It wasn't long before they'd gotten back into their usual habits.

"We've got to liven this place up," He said.

"Let's throw a party."

The thought of entertaining Steven's friends was exciting to Sherrie. She danced about, inspecting everything that the maid had done. "This gray linen, pink napkins and pink coronation centerpiece go great with this Limoges china."

"Yes, Madame. Just as you ordered," Carmella said.

"Our guest will arrive at seven-thirty," She said anxiously. "Where's that bartender?"

"The cellar, Madame. He's waiting for your instructions."

"Why didn't you tell me?" Her voice was loud but she didn't mean to hurt her feelings. "This is my first party. I want everything exquisite." She turned on her heels and hurried to the cellar

The bartender had started gathering the champagne.

"You're prompt, Mr. . ."

"Nicolas, Madame."

"Ok, Nicolas. Take two cases to the party room."

"Right behind you, Madame."

An hour later, after making sure everything was ready, Sherrie went upstairs to get dressed. She laid her blue silk gown and blue-white diamonds on the bed. Steven came in the room, held her for a moment and kissed her. "Hi, darling. Looks like you have gotten everything under control. Mind if I shower with you?"

"Ok, but no romancing." She pushed him away. "We've got guest. We must be ready."

"Spoil sport." He hit her on her derriere with his towel.

They showered and finished dressing when the doorbell rang. They descended the stairs holding hands and stood by the stairs while Laxford, the butler opened the door. The first four couples, of the fifty invited, entered the foyer. Steven greeted them, "Stanley, Erica, good to see you. Hello Andrew. Helen? You're looking gorgeous as ever." He put his arms around Sherrie and brought her closer. "Meet my new bride."

Sherrie smiled and shook their hands. "Happy to make your acquaintance."

They laughed and shook hands and after Laxford had taken the women's wraps, they went into the party room. The trio, Steven had engaged for the evening, began playing as everyone mingled. They soon began dancing as other started arriving and joined in the fun.

Sherrie whispered to Steven, "Our party is jumping."

"Yes. Nobody's going home tonight."

After the night of the party, Sherrie had gotten

on the list of the town's elite. Steven was pleased by her parties one after another. Friday night was social night ever week entertaining the country club set he called the crowd.

Sherrie enjoyed getting the party list together. "You've invited Helen this time?"

"I can't exclude her. She's one of the crowd."

"Indeed!" She said with a smirk, and watched his face out of the corner of her eye. He had that funny look when he didn't like something. He would raise the right eyebrow higher than the left and squint. She pretended not to notice, but he confronted her.

"Am I detecting a little jealousy?"

She came back at him, "Are you saying I have cause to be jealous?"

"No, but you sounded vicious."

A surge of anger pulsed through her. "Me, vicious?" She threw the party list on the floor.

"Tell me, what have you against her?" He stood in front of her and searched her face.

"Let me put it plainly." She put her hands on her hips and stared at him. "Her mouth runs like a faucet, she pretends to like Parisians and she leads Andrew around like a dog on a leash."

Without batting an eyelid, he defended her.

LOVE, PASSION AND HATE

A Faithful Choice 2

"You're wrong. She's a New Yorker that has adjusted well and Andrew's choice. That makes her all right with me."

"Why're you getting bent out of shape? Is there something going on that I should know about?"

"Don't even go there. I just don't like you putting my friends down."

"Fine. Let's add more people to the list." She put the list down in front of him.

"We can't have a party this week," He announced and moved away from her.

"I can't believe you. You're that angry with me?" She folded her arms in front of her and cleared her throat.

"I'm not. I'm going to New York. There's a buyer's convention."

"A smile creased her lips. She became excited and pleaded, "Let me come. I won't get in your way."

"It's just a meeting. You would be bored. None of the wives are going."

Her voice rose in a sharp, desperate cry, "It's her isn't it?" Her voice trembled and she stood face to face with him and stared into his eyes. "I want the truth."

"Her?" He raised his hands to the ceiling and shook his head. "You're not making any sense."

"You're taking Helen. Admit it." She demanded. "Are you leaving me for her?"

"I don't deny that I'd once been with Helen, but that was before she and Andrew married," He admitted. "It was only physical. I've never loved anyone but you."

"Liar! If you love me you'd take me with you." It seemed as if he'd turned a deaf ear to what she was saying and she was scared.

He finished packing, locked the suitcase, and gave her a quick kiss. He hurried down the stairs and out the front door.

Sherrie heard the tires of Steven's ruby red Astin Martin squeal as he backed out of the driveway. And she ran to the window, watched the car speed down the street and out of sight. Her man was leaving her behind. She sat on the bed and cried uncontrollably. Several hours went by and she was still sitting and drying her eyes. Then she got up, went to the bathroom and sat on the toilet. When she had finished, she couldn't get up. She felt paralyzed and sat thirty minutes before trying again. With both hands on the toilet seat, she thrust her right foot in front of her, pushed with her left and propelled herself to stand.

LOVE, PASSION AND HATE

A Faithful Choice 2

All of her energy had been drained, but she walked slowly to the den, sat at the bar and poured a tall glass of Chardonnay. The telephone rang and she was a little tipsy when she answered. "Mama?" She struggled to hold back more tears and a large lump arose in her throat as she pursed her lips when a tear ran down her cheek. "Steven went to New York. He left me behind."

"I'm at the chateau. Come and stay with your grand mother."

Sherrie gathered her clothes and threw them in the backseat of her silver Mercedes. She arrived at Dolores' chateau and fell into her arms. "I'm shaken; I feel whipped." She tearfully laid her head on Dolores' bosom. "I love Steven, Grand-mamma, in spite of his faults."

"Don't fret. If you want to go to New York take Christy's place. She has her hands full with the twins."

"Grand-mamma, you always know how to solve our problems."

"How is that going to solve anything with you there and him here?" Michelle asked. "He's going to return."

He should've taken me."

"That's beside the point. Stay here until he

106

returns."

"I'll not beg for his attention. I can do something on my own. Why do I have to wait for him?"
"Don't do anything stupid, Sherrie," Michelle said. "You married a Fodor."

"We didn't try to talk you out of it, though his father hates our family." Dolores said.

"Steven is not like his father," Sherrie said. "He doesn't hold grudges."

"Let's hope he doesn't turn into Martin," Michelle said. "When there's money involved, people change."

A Faithful Choice 2

CHAPTER 10

Sherrie arrived in New York, went directly to Dolores' house and got settled in her mother's old room. She made a call to Paris. "I'm here. I'll go to Velasco's early in the morning." The next call was to Steven. "I'm here in New York."

"What? Are you checking up on me?"

"Everything is not about you, Steven. I promised Grand-mamma to do some work at Velasco's"

"How long will that take?"

"I don't know. Six months or more. Depends."

"What am I suppose to do? You here. Me in Paris."

"You didn't have any qualms leaving me."

"It was business."

"This is business, also." She heard his intake of breath and the fury in his voice.

"I've got to go. Got another meeting. Talk to you later."

"Fine." She placed the phone in its receiver, undressed and into her pajamas. Sleep did not come until three in the morning. She lied there thinking of

Steven and how she was not going to be ruled by him. She was her own person, a strong and intelligent woman, and she had certain wants and needs. He would just have to accept that what she wanted was important too.

The alarm clock sounded at seven in the morning. Oh, if she could sleep another hour, Sherrie though and rolled out of bed. A cup of coffee and a piece of toast gave her a little strength to shower and dress. Seven-fifty, she was out of the door and Herman was driving her down the streets of Manhattan, nearing 34th Street. He drove into the garage and parked in Leonard Velasco's spot. "Should I pick you up at the usual time?"

"Yes, Herman." The ride on the elevator to the third floor almost rocked her back to sleep. When she stepped off the elevator, a short, dark, gray bearded man approached her. "You must be Mrs. Brown's grand daughter, Mrs. Sherrie Fodor." He extended his hand. "Bob Green. Welcome."

"Mr. Green, You've been with the company for thirty years. Nice to see you."

"Yes. I can't bring myself to retire," he said, still shaking his head when he talked, which now, seemed as if he had Bell's palsy. He escorted her to Dolores's office. "Here you are." He stopped in front of the first office.

"Thanks, Mr. Green." She sat in the cushioned chair behind the mahogany desk, just as her grandmamma did when she first came there. She swiveled the chair around a couple of times, thinking that this must've been an accomplishment in Grand mamma's day. She felt cool and confident as her derriere sank in the thick, brown leather chair. She fumbled the papers in the tray on the desk and read a few. Revenues were up. The store was doing great and she would make sure that it stayed that way. She would keep it on a steady course just as Grand mamma did years earlier, and she reached for the file that contained a list of the employees and the phone.

"Mr. Green, I'd like to call a meeting in the next hour."

"Right away." He hurried down the hall to get things rolling.

They gathered in the conference room and took a seat at the large mahogany table with seating for ten. Jerry Rogers, the manager, his three assistants, Bob Green, the coordinator and his assistant, Julienne. They were all pleasant and Sherrie found herself warming to them as she made her proposals known. "I want to change the store's four windows. They must be well-dressed, eye-catching, professionally done with the latest fashions." She picked the best woman the store had. "Julienne? You were one of the top models here."

"She's well informed about fashion," Bob Green said, handing her the rundown on current sales and the latest figures. "She's my number one assistant."

110

"Who did we hire for the window dresser?"

"Paul Seitz," Bob said. He's the best in the business."

"I'll give him a call, later."

Julienne handed a few sketches of cocktail suites with ruffles on the jacket, ¾ inch sleeves and portrait collar, three piece cascade sets with ruffled lapel over a sleeveless lace top, in white, with black knit pants and a few lace print dresses in a figure-flattering black knit print.

"I like the suites. The skirt streamlines the look."

"Yes. It's flattering, feminine, and sexy in shimmering teal," Bob said.

"I like the way it clings to the body." Julienne said.

Sherrie gave her nod of approval, and at the end of an hour, she dismissed everyone to converse with Paul Seitz; bending his ear to her satisfaction and waiting for his staff to begin the window dressing. Three hours later, she stood in front of the windows, with him, studying the clothing on the dummies. "I like it. Those gladiator shoes by Channel are beautiful."

"Top of the line," he said. "It's a whole new look."

"What's the top?"

LOVE, PASSION AND HATE

A Faithful Choice 2

"$1,525.00 a pair."

She nodded emphatically. "Sensational! You've outdone yourself."

He gave her a delighted grin and a hand shake.

It was late when Sherrie got home and when she entered the door, the phone rang. She answered when she saw Steven's number. "Hello. How was your day?"

"Could've been better. I need to be with you."

"I'm not going anywhere. Come over."

Within minutes, Steven arrived. He rushed inside and took her in his arms. "I've missed your gorgeous body next to mine." He picked her up and took her to the bedroom. They lay in bed and he kissed her passionately and gently. "You're dynamic." He slid his tongue slowly and sensually into her mouth. Their bodies mingled as one. It was pure ecstasy. He rolled over on his side and gave her an affectionate slap on the rump, then sat up in bed, lit a cigarette and lay back on his pillow.

She gazed at his wide, muscular, hairy chest, strong arms and large masculine feet. He was still the most desirable man she'd ever met. He was everything she ever dreamed of, and it was impossible to stay angry with him long. Everything about him was irresistibly charming. He was a fun guy, terrific in bed, still good-looking, and he loved to have a good time.

"When are you returning to Paris?"

"I'm staying over, until you return with me."

"What about the mill?"

"Dad is fully capable of taking care of things. Life is lonely and boring by one's-self."

As much as I love having you with me, you're going to get bored not working."

"I can take a break and so can you. Working the entire time makes one a dull person. Besides, just because your grand mother worked obsessively, doesn't mean you have to do the same."

She leaned forward, her face growing angry. "Ok. I see what're you're doing."

"What?" He gave her a puzzling stare.

"You're trying to persuade me to return to Paris."

"It seems to me you're taking on too many projects above your head."

She jumped off the bed and stood with her hands on her hips, her indignation surfacing. "How could you say such a thing? How dare you act as if my career doesn't matter."

He arranged a pleasant smile on his face and said, "I'm sorry, but if you're here, we may as well not be married, for all the times we will see each other, and the little time we'll spend together."

"It's just until I get everything organized here."

"But your sister-in-law has done all of the organizing."

Her voice grew softer and she put her arms around him. "Things change. Velasco's have to keep up with the trends. Besides, I promised Grand-Mamma."

"What about your promises to me? We're married. I need you home. Can't you do all of this at the store in Paris?"

She held steady, her jaw firm and shook her head. "Maybe later. Not now."

"I married you because you keep me going. You challenge me. I challenge you. We push each other to do the right thing."

"I have a voice, Steven, and I demand to be heard."

"You're being heard. That's what we're discussing now."

She stomped her foot and met his eyes head on. "I can't go back to Paris just yet."

"Can't or won't?"

"Call it what you like. I'm needed here."

"Is it more important to meet the needs here than my needs?"

"You're being unreasonable, stating it like that."

"Whatever. I have a meeting to attend and then I'm returning to Paris." He gave her a long hard stare. "I'll wait for you at the airport if you decide to come. Three o'clock." He packed his things and left, without as much as a kiss goodbye.

Her heart sank and she dialed her mother's number. "Mama? Steven wants me to forget everything and come back to Paris."

"Don't do something that you may regret. You should be with your husband."

"Things are not going with us the way that I expected."

"I admit I was against your marriage to a Fodor, but now, you and Steven should stay together. Solve your problems and compromise."

She couldn't believe her mother was siding with him. Her hopes were flattened. Her family didn't like the Fodor's. "You're saying I should give up my career for the sake of my marriage?"

"Ask yourself what's more important. Your father and I went through this. Believe me; you should

115

LOVE, PASSION AND HATE

A Faithful Choice 2

be here with your husband."

"I'll finish here and come later." She sat on the bed and sighed. Her dreams of working in New York were shattered, her hopes, compromised.

LOVE, PASSION AND HATE

A Faithful Choice 2

CHAPTER 11

Steven arose early and went to the mill. His father greeted him, "Glad to see you home, son."

"I had to come back, Father. I know you needed my help."

"Did your wife come back with you?"

"No. She's still in New York."

"So, she's forsaken you. I knew when you married her she was just like the rest of them."

"Let's not go there, Father. I don't care for you speaking of her that way."

"I'm sorry, but those Glauerts are no good."

"I don't wish to hear another word about my in-laws." He moved away from him. "Besides, you're not blameless in what happened with our mill."

His mouth came agape and he became indignant. "Whatever do you mean?"

"I know the whole story. Let's just forget about faults."

"I'll come over and cook for you, Son," Carissa said.

"There's no need, Mom, besides I intend to

make Sherrie an offer she can't refuse."

"How exciting! What are you planning?"

"I'm going to offer her a position at the mill."

"Are you crazy?" Martin shouted. "I won't have another Glauert in my presence or in my mill."

"The last time I viewed my marriage license, Sherrie's last name is Fodor and you forget, half this mill is mine."

"She's not blood."

"She's my wife and that's as good as blood." He stormed out and went home.

"Please, Martin, don't drive our son away."

"He's been brainwashed by those lying, cheating people and I'm not going to stand by and wait for them to take my mill away."

"Martin? What are you going to do?" The rage in his eyes frightened her. "Don't do anything you'll regret.
"Never mind, Carissa, you stick to your ladies' club and bazaars. I'll do the thinking for us."

"Martin, where are you going?"

"I'm going to put a stop to these thieves." He hurried to his green Mercedes and drove away causing his tires to squeal and burn rubber. He sped ahead, running through lights, not waiting for the light to change green and darting in and out of cars as he continue to speed. He paid no attention to the angry drivers when they gave him the finger.

Sherrie's phone rang and she answered. The time displayed one a.m., but no caller's number showed on the screen. She heard breathing. "Who is this?" Still no one said anything. "Jackass," She shouted, slammed the phone in its receiver and turned over in bed. She twisted and turned until she fell asleep.

As usual, the alarm clock sounded at 7 o'clock that morning, and she slowly slid out of bed. After eating, she was out the door within an hour. Herman drove into the garage at Velasco's, turned around and let her out near the elevator. Out of the corner of her eye, seconds before she stepped on the elevator, she noticed a tall, stocky man wearing black pants and a black hoodie. He hurried toward the elevator and she held her finger on the button for the third floor. Her gut feeling told her that he was up to no good and she was not going to wait around to prove herself right or wrong.

She stepped off the elevator and hurried to her office to find Bob Green sitting in a chair waiting for her. "Anything wrong?"

"Today is the day for the fashion show." He answered appearing anxious.

"Are the models lined up?"

"Julienne has scheduled the show for noon and the designers are ready to go."

"This evening is going to be a unique experience." She felt the buzz, the sense of excitement, the undercurrent of anticipation and a feeling that this show would be the event of the season.

"We have the rich and famous; elegance personified," He said. "The crowd in the lounge is the crème de la crème of New York's fashion society."

"I didn't expect so many and at noon." She smiled and popped her fingers. "This showing has a great collection."

"You have excellent choices." He exuded great confidence in his voice. "It's going to be your day. Just like your grand mother."

She smiled, closed her eyes and tossed her hair over her shoulders. "And my year." She felt more confident that she'd made the right decision to stay in New York and not to return to Paris. "Grand-mamma would be proud." She rushed to the dressing room to get ready and pulled her shocking pink cocktail dress from the hanger, slipped into it and slid her feet into the black satin stilettoes. Within a few seconds, she headed for the lounge down the hall from the dressing room and spotted a few buyers that she had previously met when she first arrived at Velasco's. "Velma, nice to see you." She greeted her with an affectionate hug "Louis, you're looking debonair," She said watching him cling

A Faithful Choice 2

to Velma. She walked inside as the press entered and she posed with a glass of champagne in her hand and her arm around Elizabeth Ross, a distinguished buyer of quality high fashion. She stepped up on the stage, positioned the microphone and greeted everyone. "Ladies and Gentleman, I have an excellent array of fashions that I am sure will more than excite you." She waved her hand toward the designers. "I want to introduce Velasco's brilliant designers who are responsible for what you will see today. So sit back and be prepared to be mesmerized."

Five models descended on the runway. The first wearing a tailored, pale blue silk suit, and a white chiffon blouse. The crowd clapped and Sherrie beamed. "Next we have street style. These ladies stay fashionable despite frigid temperatures, wearing layers, leggings and chunky knits. A tan car coat of suede with a red fox collar, chunky black knitted top over a long tan knit skirt." She looked at the crowd and everyone was smiling. "Next we have black skin tight leather tights with suede boots and a black wool sweater with a black fox collar and cuffs."

The crowd went wild with applause and Sherrie continued, "We have a sleeveless black and white dress with a matching top coat. It's cashmere and silk, but made in America ladies and gentleman, by Victor Coterie, right here at Velasco's. Now for the show stoppers: Our purple silk dress with a princess line skirt,

121

beautifully embroidered with pearls and a sequined neckline; truly a sensational item."

The models danced off the stage and four others entered. "This ladies and gentleman is an off white silk tuxedo top with black lapels and black slit pockets over black silk tights. Number three is wearing an emerald silk gown, flared in the back at the hemline. Number four is wearing a knee high black leather skirt with a diamond studded weskit and a black long sleeve silk blouse. All of these items can be purchased in our store and by special order. So, please, ladies and gentlemen do stop by Valesco's and place your order. These end our fashion show, and now, let's enjoy the delicacies that I ordered especially for this accession and the cocktails."

Everyone descended on the food trays in the next room and Sherrie moved among the crowd to hear their comments on the fashions. "I should record these comments." She was about to go to her office and Juliann stopped her.

Relax. I'll get the recorder for you." She headed for Sherrie's office and walked into darkness. She clicked the switch several times and heard a noise. "Hello. Is anyone there?" She was about to turn around and leave when she was knocked to the floor and she felt a large fist slam into her stomach, then a large foot kicking her in the head. She screamed, "Stop, please, don't kill me." But she felt the damming blow against her head, one after another until two large hands grabbed her throat. She could feel herself loosing consciousness and she made one last effort to save herself by kicking the assailant in his groin, which gave her a moment to catch her breath as he fell backward

and released the pressure on her throat. "God, please help me." She began crawling toward the door when she heard Sherrie's voice.

"Julianne? Where's the recorder? What's taking so long?" She tried the switch and tripped over Julianne's body. She screamed, "My Lord! Help! Someone…anyone… help."

Bob Green rushed inside. Wait. I have a flashlight."

They stared at Julianne as blood gushed from her nose. "Call 911," Sherrie screamed.

When the ambulance arrived, Sherrie hopped inside after they loaded Julianne and the stretcher into the ambulance. She held her hand as tears flooded her cheeks. "Hold on, Julianne. Don't you die on me." Her thoughts drifted to her grandmother. "What will I tell Grand-mamma? Please, Julianne, stay with me." She said a prayer. "Please, Lord, Don't let her die. You've always answered my prayers. Please hear me now." She hopped out of the ambulance when it stopped in the emergency lane at Cedars Mt. Sinai, and followed them to the information desk and to triage." This is my employee. Do everything you can for her. Don't spare the expense." She placed a call to her grandmother. "Now, don't get upset, but Julianne is in the emergency room at Cedars Mt. Sinai." She swallowed hard, suddenly realizing that she was the intended victim. "Someone mistook her for me."

"Sherrie, thank God, you're ok, and Julianne, is she going to pull through?"

"I don't know. She was badly beaten."

"Keep me informed. Should I come to New York?"

"Not yet. Wait until I talk to the doctors."

"There are many enemies out there," Dolores said. Be careful."

"I'll be careful." She finished talking with Dolores and dialed Steven's phone. "Someone tried to kill Julianne in my office. I'm certain that they thought she was me."

"You've got to come home." Steven said out of breath. "I need to keep you safe."

"I'm fine. Security is all over the place."

"Yet they managed to get Julianne. I'm getting a flight this minute. Dad can handle things here."

LOVE, PASSION AND HATE

A Faithful Choice 2

"No. Don't come. Please, it's not necessary."

"Get a gun. Will you do that for me?"

"I don't like guns. Besides, I wouldn't know how to shoot one."

"Ok. Hire a body guard."

"I'll hire one tomorrow. I have to go. The police are here to talk with me."

"I'm Detective Pier Bonner." He shook her hand. "What happened? I need the facts."

"I'm Sherrie Fodor. My employee was attacked when she went to my office at Velasco's."

"Apparently, you were the intended victim. I'd like to assign one of my men to you, in your office and at your home."

"Thank you, Detective. I greatly appreciate your concern."

"Is there anything you can add…something that occurred to you before this?"

"I believed that I was followed, but I'm not sure."

"Could you give a description of the person?"

"No. I wish---." She held her head. "He was wearing a black hoodie."

"Never mind, I'll put several men on the case, and I'll come to your office and take a look." He shook his head and a strand of red hair flipped onto his forehead. "I appreciate you being so cooperative."

"Is there anything else?"

"Not for now. I'll be in touch. We'll do everything to find the suspect."

After Sherrie had sat with Julianne for an hour, she called Herman to take her home. They were two blocks before turning to get to Dolores' house when a black Chevrolet with tinted windows fell in behind and followed them. "There seems to be someone following us," Herman said, peering through the rear view mirror. "I'm going to go through this yellow light." He raced through the light and the driver of the Chevrolet busted the red light to keep up, then jammed on his breaks and sped up as soon as he was cleared of the light. "I'm taking this abrupt right turn without using my blinker." The Chevrolet raced past the turn and pulled to the curb. "I know a different street to take from here. Don't worry, he won't catch us."

When they reached the house, the two assigned squad cars were parked outside. They got out of their cars when Herman pulled into the driveway. "I'm Detective Byrd. My partner, Delaney."

LOVE, PASSION AND HATE

A Faithful Choice 2

"We were chased a couple of blocks before arriving here," Sherrie said.

"Did you get the license plate number?"

"Sorry, no. They were driving too fast."

"Ok. Don't worry. We're out here."

"Uh-uh." She shook her head. "That's comforting to know." She excused herself and went inside. Sleep wasn't going to be easy tonight; the thought of someone trying to kill her and so close to home unnerved her. She sat up and looked at television for three hours, hoping to get herself in the mood for sleep. When nothing happened, she dressed in her pajamas and got in bed. She lay there for hours and finally at three in the morning she closed her eyes and fell asleep.

The next morning, she was like a zombie. A cup of coffee and a slice of dry toast was all that she could handle. It took her two hours to get dressed for the office before she called Herman. He picked her up and had only gone three blocks when the black Chevrolet pulled out of a side street in front of them. He had probably been searching the area, waiting for them to drive where they had left him. She placed a call to Detective Byrd. "That car that I told you about is following me."

"I'm on the way."

Detective Byrd was there in five minutes. He spotted him and chased him. The Chevrolet ran, but Byrd pushed after him hard, closing the gap. He had turned into a cul-de-sac. He was trapped. Shots were fired. The driver's window was down and he was firing his gun. "Get out of the car. Keep your hands where I can see them," Detective Byrd yelled. The door opened. He raised his hand and walked slowly out towards Byrd. He was tall, muscular and heavy set. He wore his hair in long black dreadlocks. His eyes were dark and menacing. "On your knees," Byrd said. "Fingers locked behind your head."

Delaney cuffed him and put him in the back of the squad car. "We're taking him to the 19th precinct on 153 East 67th Street. We'll let you know why he was chasing you."

She tried to smile but her lips were dry and her tongue felt as if it was stuck to the floor of her mouth. "Let's get out of here, Herman. I've got to get to work." When he let her out in the garage, she stepped slowly onto the elevator and walked somberly to her office. She didn't want to think about the situation with this man trying to kill her. It was an attempted murder investigation and questions had to be asked, but she was hoping to avoid anything the police came up with; pretend that it all was a mistake and that it would go away.

Two hours later, her office phone buzzed. She stared at it as it buzzed again and glanced at the number, then answered, "Sherrie Fodor."

"Mrs. Fodor? Detective Byrd, here. The suspect is a two time looser, jailed on drugs, mugging and stealing." He took a deep breath and continued, "His name is Tommy Brown and he refused to tell who hired him to kill you. He's going back to jail."

She became nauseous and felt the sting of acid on the back of her tongue. She grew irritated and confused and suddenly scared. Who was out to get her? She hadn't done anything to anyone. They were ruining her career and she would soon have to go back to Paris. Someone was watching her and she didn't want to stay around to find out who hated her to the point of wanting her dead. She called Steven. "I'm coming home. I won't be able to work in peace knowing that someone wants me dead."

"It's for the best. I'll meet you at the airport."

Julianne came out of the hospital, after three weeks and she had recovered. Dolores gave her a raise and a welcome back party.

A Faithful Choice 2

CHAPTER 12

Sherrie was home for two weeks before she
began to feel safe. She went to bed early and slept late.
Steven came home early to be with her. "I have a
proposition for you. Work with me at the mill."

"I'm not a mill person. If I wanted to work at a
mill, I could do so for my Father."

"We can spend time together. Think about
working with me."

She kicked the floor. "Man, I knew you'd think
of something to get me to stay here." She rubbed her
forehead in circular strokes.

"It's for you so you can stop feeling afraid."

I really don't need this." She palmed her
forehead. "God, I don't know what I'm doing here. I
had a good job." Little by little, she felt her control
slipping from her. "I have to talk with Grand-mamma."
She got into her silver Mercedes and drove past the
speed limit of twenty-five miles. The light was green,
and then quickly turned yellow. A couple of drivers
honked their horns and gave her the finger and she
barely waited for the light to turn green before she sped
past the other drivers.

Michelle and Dolores hugged her in a tight grip,

after she entered the chateau.

"Are you alright?" Dolores asked. "We've put together a surprise welcoming home party for you, tonight, but if you'd rather be alone---."

"No. I need to be with my family."

"What have you done to find the culprit?" Michelle rubbed her back as she did when she was a baby. "Have you contacted the police here?"

"Steven is taking care of everything." Tears spilled down her face, wetting her green blouse. "What am I suppose to do now? I need my work."

"Get yourself together, first, then, worry about a job." Dolores said. "You can work in the Paris office. I'm sure James would welcome the help."

"You'll be fine." Michelle patted her hand. "We'll just have to pray harder for you."

"We'll get through this together." Dolores sat close to her, hugged her shoulders. "God kept you from being murdered. He'll keep you now. Have faith."

"I've been trying. It's hard." Sherrie hated the whiney sound of her voice. She'd always been strong. Nothing deterred her or unnerved her. She was falling apart. She bit her lower lip. "I'm going to fight this thing or person, who wants me dead."

Michelle raised her fist. "We're unbreakable.

A Faithful Choice 2

No one messes with the Glauerts and the Browns."

"I'll give my answer to Steven today. He wants me to work at the mill."

"Working with crazy Martin?" Michelle yelled. "You'll be in a worse environment."

Steven seems to think we need time together and he can protect me."

"I applaud Steven, but Martin is another animal." Michelle couldn't stop her eyes from rolling and shaking her shoulders, marking Martin.

Sherrie couldn't stop laughing. She forgot about her troubles for a moment. "I can go home and forget about this mess."

"Call if you need us," Dolores said. "We'll be there in a flash."

Sherrie went home and got in bed.

Steven came home and sat on the bed. "How was your day?"

"Could you not speak? My head's about to explode."

He got off the bed, and then closed the door. She knew she sounded like a bitch, but his voice raked her nerves.

Steven reentered the room carrying a tray of steak, potato salad and coffee. He pointed to the chase lounger in the corner by the window. "I'll sit here. I promise not to talk." He placed the tray on the bed and headed for the lounger.

She rose up and placed a hand on his forearm. "I'm sorry. Come on, get in bed." She kissed his lips softly. "This nightmare of someone trying to kill me…."

"I know. That's why I'm going to protect you."

"How?"

"Don't worry." He moved closer to her side and cradled her in his arms. "I'm taking care of everything." He got out of bed and hurried toward the door. "I have to leave for an hour. Go to sleep."

When Steven left, Sherrie felt jittery and got out of bed. She tried to ignore the knots tightening her stomach. She heard a noise and turned around. "You scared the….! How'd you get in here?"

"You left the door unlocked."

Crazy-ass bitch…! She thought, wondering why she was getting a visit from her nut-case of a mother-in-law. Be nice, she told herself. "Would you like some tea?"

"I'll get it for you. Relax. We haven't said too much to one another. I'm here to remedy that mistake." She went to the kitchen, prepared the tea, returned and

133

placed it in her hand.

Sherrie sipped the tea until the cup was empty, and Carissa watched her with an evil look in her eye. "I must complete what I've come here to do. That's it go to sleep. The medicine will take effect in seconds."

"What have you done to me?" Lightness enveloped her head, a dribble of saliva trickled on to her chin and she felt herself losing consciousness. After a few moments, she felt herself sinking into a deep sleep.

"Don't fear this. It isn't going to hurt." She helped her to lie down on the soft. "That's it. Nice and easy. I know my son believes he loves you, but he's blinded by your deception." She started undressing her. "My husband use to be happy and he treated me like a queen. You Glauerts turned him into a domineering, angry, frustrated man." She felt herself letting go of the hate filled tension inside of her, and she leaned back on the sofa and cried uncontrollably, then got up. "I'm sorry but I can't lose Steven and Martin. She composed a note. "I love you, Steven, but I can't live with the fear. You can have my part of the mill. I don't need it."

Sherrie felt heavy hands clamping her shoulders and hauling her to her feet. Her butt smacked the bottom of the bathtub and cold water soaked her body as Carissa filled the tub with water.

"I'm sorry, but your death is better for my family. You Glauerts are destroyers of decent, loving people." She pushed Sherrie's head down into the tub. "I was a lucky woman to be married to Martin. He's a good man who has always cared for his family."

Sherrie stopped fighting for air as the water enveloped her face, nose and hair, listening to her murderer. The door whipped open. She heard shots, the crack of the bullets, someone emptying their gun, screams and heavy hands pulling her out of the tub, someone's mouth on her mouth; filling her lungs with air.

Steven ran inside. "Oh, my God! Mom? You did this? Why?"

"I did this for you and your father. Please, don't hate me." She coughed, blood trickled from her mouth and nose and she was gone.

Sherrie? Say something. Please, darling, speak to me."

"Steven? What happened? Your mom…"

"I know." Tears trickled down his cheeks and fell onto her face. "I hired a body guard for you. I never imagined that I was hiring my mother's killer."

She could feel the pain on his face but all she could think of was how much she loved him and happy to be alive.

"I must call Dad…let him know." He telephoned Martin. "Get here as fast as you can. I need you." He got a robe and covered Sherrie's naked body.

Martin arrived when the police and the coroners arrived. "What's going on?" He looked at Carissa's body lying still and bleeding on the floor and he sank to his knees beside her. "What happened?"

Steven wanted to spare him but he had to tell him. "Mom tried to kill Sherrie."

"No!" His mournful shriek filled the room. "Son of a---Why?" Curse words rolled off his tongue, and tumbled off his lips as he held her in his arms. "I should've been more sensitive to her needs, more loving. I'm as guilty as she."

The coroner had to pry Martin's arms from Carissa's body. "Excuse me, Sir. We must remove the body."

"Who shot her?" Martin asked. "God help her. She needed me."

"I hired detective Louis Waylon of the police force. He kept surveillance on this house."

"How am I going to live without her?" A wild

mixture of hysteria and loneliness rioted his mind. "Why did she have to die like this?" He didn't look at Sherrie. He lowered his head and walked swiftly to the door. "I've got to get out of here."

"Dad, Wait. Stay here. Let us help you."

"No! I've got to be alone."

Sherrie extended her hand to him, looked up into his deep scowl, and then stepped back. "I'm sorry for your loss."

He headed out the door and didn't look back.

Steven watched him march away. "He'll be ok. I'll check on him tomorrow."

"If you want to go with him, I'll be alright."

"No. My place is here with you." He held her close, thanking God that she was alive. "If you want to go back to New York, I won't object."

"No. I'll have plenty to do here in the Paris office. My place is here with you. I love you, Steven." She drew in a deep breath and clung to him. "I'm going to stay here, love my man and one day raise his children."

"I could definitely get use to that," He said and kissed her.

THE END

30073481R00085

Made in the USA
Charleston, SC
04 June 2014